Crazy

About

Horses

Crazy

About

Horses

BY

SHANNON GARST

WITH ILLUSTRATIONS BY

WESLEY DENNIS

HASTINGS HOUSE, PUBLISHERS, NEW YORK

Library of Congress Catalog Card Number: 57-10737

Published simultaneously in Canada by
S. J. Reginald Saunders, Publishers, Toronto 2B

Printed in the United States of America

TO THAT SPECIAL "TOP HAND"

Charles Joseph Spurlock

CONTENTS

Crazy

About

Horses

CHAPTER I

A Challenge to Meet

DAVE BRANDT stepped from the train at the small station called Longhorn and stared about. The porter piled his suitcases around him. "I reckon someone'll come along directly and pick you up," he said uncertainly.

"Yes, of course they will. My uncle knows I'm coming," Dave said.

"Folks hardly ever expects this train to be on time," the porter explained. "That's most likely why your folks aren't here already."

"I suppose so," Dave said. "They'll be along. I'm not worried." He made himself speak with an ease of manner and an assurance that he didn't feel. In fact, he had quite a sinking of the heart as he stared around at the dreary scene: the station with faded peeling mustard-colored paint; the drooping shacks that lined the alley facing the depot. There was a small plot of ground beside the

11

station. The plot obviously had been intended to be a lawn but it had long ago given over to weeds and blown páper.

The town was such a small place; merely a huddle of stores lining an unpaved street. Probably beyond the stores were a few houses, but those he had seen from the train window were as small and dreary looking as the station and shacks and sheds facing the track. He had lived all of his twelve years in Chicago and had never been in such a small place before.

The train whistled.

"All aboard!" shouted the conductor, although no one was there to get on.

The train pulled out leaving Dave an island of desolation amid his luggage. What would he do,

he wondered, if no one came to meet him? Oh, but surely they would! There had been some delay. He sat down on one of his suitcases to wait, the feeling of chilled disappointment still hard upon him. He hadn't known just what he had expected, yet it was nothing like this. Why, there wasn't even a cowboy in sight, in spite of the town's rather romantic name of "Longhorn." If this was a typical cowtown, he wanted none of it.

He was suddenly a homesick, lonely boy with nowhere to go. The wind that whistled across the empty prairie chilled him to the bone. He yanked his wide hat over his ears, raised the collar of his leather jacket, and hunched himself up and hugged himself with his arms.

Just then a jeep came careening up the street and with a screeching of brakes stopped close to where Dave sat forlornly on one of his suitcases.

A character with chin whiskers and skin the color and texture of a dried potato peered at him from under a greasy-brimmed cowboy hat. "Hi, young fella!" came out a scratchy voice that somehow matched the man's seedy appearance. "Be you Dave Brandt? Sure you be. I'd know you anywheres. You've got the Brandt cowlick, the long nose, and same ears set close to your head like a prairie dog's. And that's pretty nifty cowboy rigging you're wearing—even to the ten-gallon hat and fancy, high-heeled boots."

Dave stood up and looked the stranger over. "My uncle Bill Brandt was going to meet me here. I'm going to his Rocking B Ranch to work."

A cackle came from the whiskers. "Work! Hunh! Well, that's yore uncle's problem, I reckon. He sent me to meet you. Happens all hands is busy branding today. Couldn't spare me. But someone had to come. So here I am. Dump yore luggage in the back of the jeep and climb aboard. Old Leaping Lena here will make the trip in two jumps."

He patted the steering wheel as he spoke. Dave guessed that "Leaping Lena" was his name for the battered vehicle.

He was surprised that the man did not help him put the suitcases in the jeep; obviously he was a hired man on Uncle Bill's cattle ranch. Obviously, too, he was a very independent person.

Dave climbed up onto the seat and with a snort the jeep backed around with a speed that made Dave's heart miss a beat. Then they were off through the small town, which Dave now saw had some neat but modest frame houses with flowers in the yards. Perhaps, he thought, this might not be such a bad place after all if you didn't mind living in a postage stamp of a town.

They passed through the village quickly and the driver of the jeep gave Dave an extra thrill or so when he deliberately tried to hit a few chickens pecking along the road. The cracked laughter that came from the depths of his gray beard sounded to Dave very like the outraged cackles of the nearly-run-over chickens.

"Dratted fussy critters! Never did like chickens," Graybeard confided to Dave as they spurted forth toward the blue mountains. Those mountains gave Dave the first lift of heart he had felt since he had stepped off the train. Maybe life wouldn't be so dreary and desolate out on the ranch near those mountains as it must be in the small, unattractive town they were leaving.

"My name's Jackson," the graybeard said. "But everyone calls me Windy. On account of because I talk so much, I reckon. Tongue waggles on both ends, they tell me." He chuckled.

"I'm happy to know you, Mr. Jackson," Dave said. "My father and Uncle Bill are brothers."

The withered face turned toward him, and Dave felt that he was being carefully studied. "Ain't much I don't know about you, young fella," Windy said. "You've been a bit of a problem to your dad at home. Reckon he's too busy counting oil royalties to pay much attention to a young un. So you got to running wild. You flunked a grade at school. So what does Papa do? Just what a lot of rich dads do—dump their problem kids on some unlucky relative that lives on a cattle ranch. As if people who run ranches didn't have enough to do without riding herd on spoiled city brats."

Dave stiffened, feeling as if he had been plunged into icy water. He was angry through and through. "Stop the jeep," he said in a voice that trembled. "Stop this minute, I say! I had a feeling all along that Dad was sending me out here to get me off his hands. But I didn't know I was going to be so much trouble to Uncle Bill. Stop! Let me off!"

Windy reached up with one hand and stroked his beard without slackening the speed of the jeep. "There I go again," he said ruefully. "Shooting the breeze. Opening my big mouth and putting my foot in it. I didn't mean for what I said to sound the way it did. Honest I didn't. I was just ramblin' on, the way I do. Most folks is used to me."

"I still want you to stop the jeep and let me out." Cold fury tinged Dave's voice.

"What you figger to do? Walk back to town with all that fancy luggage o' yourn?"

"Somebody'll be along and pick me up," Dave said.

Again one hand reached up to tug the beard.

"I'm not stoppin' for two reasons," the old man said. "I don't take orders from anybody but the boss. His orders was to bring you to the ranch. Secondly, if I let you off I'd have to let the boss know why and he'd be so doggoned mad he'd fire me. You don't want to get an old friend in wrong, do you?"

"You're not my friend and I don't much care what happens to you," Dave said.

"Oh, come now! I admit I was a goldarned fool to spill the beans the way I did. I just talk without thinking. Likely you'll find I'm one of your best friends before the summer's over. Just simmer down now and enjoy the scenery. The Rocking B lies just under those blue mountains. The prettiest spread you ever did see."

Dave sat stiffly in dignified silence, but at last the peace and serenity of the landscape eased his heart. How could anyone remain angry when meadowlarks burst into song at every turn of the road? Where jackrabbits bounded from the sagebrush, and where an antelope browsing beside the road merely lifted his head and stared curiously but did not run? Farther on was a small herd of does and fawns grazing in a meadow.

"Oh, I'm going to like this!" Dave cried, his hurt and anger forgotten.

"Sure you be," Windy said. Then in his cracked voice he started to sing:

"Home, home on the range,
  Where the deer and the antelope play—"

As the sound of his off-key voice, the animals raised their heads and bounded away with long, bouncy steps.

Both Dave and Windy broke into laughter at this unexpected effect of Windy's singing.

"You can't expect wild animals to appreciate good music," Windy chuckled, but continued singing, undiscouraged, and Dave joined in.

"That's my boy." The old man turned to grin at him. "You aren't mad at me no more. I want you to like me. I really do."

"I like you." Dave said it grudgingly, yet he couldn't help feeling drawn to the absurd old fellow. "After all, you told me the truth. I knew it without being told. I guess it's the truth that hurts. But I don't want to be a nuisance. I know that Uncle Bill's busy. I'd really hoped to learn to be a regular cowboy so that I could help him out."

"You've come to the right man to help you learn cowboyin' fast, meaning *me!*" Windy said, and launched into a long monologue of the wonderful things he had done on the range and at rodeos. To hear him tell it, there was no one his equal in the entire West.

Dave let him ramble on, not believing such preposterous tales and busy with his own thoughts of how he would immediately prove himself to be a top hand on the range. His own daydreams were more entertaining to him than Windy's bragging.

At last they came to a fork in the road where there was a large swinging gate with a cattle guard beside it. Over the gate was a pair of sweeping steer horns and under them, carved into a wide board, was ⚓B, the Rocking B brand, Windy explained.

As they bumped over the cattle guard, Dave's heart began to beat fast. This was it! A real Wyoming cattle ranch. The summer was going to be fun and exciting—and successful. He would see to that. His uncle wouldn't be sorry he had come. Dave would make him and his dad proud of him. He would prove that he had the makings of a top hand. He didn't know just how he would accomplish it, but he was determined. This, he realized, was the first real challenge of his life. Here the fact that he was a rich man's son wouldn't mean a thing—in fact, it might be something he had to live down.

Dust was rising from one of the corrals. "They're not through with the branding yet," Windy said. "I knew they wouldn't be able to finish before sundown without my help."

Dave jumped down. "Can I do anything to help?" he asked eagerly.

"Nope," Windy said. "You'd likely just get in the way. Grab yourself a seat on the opery bench up there." With a wave of the hand he indicated the top row of the pole corral.

Dave climbed up and hooked the high pointed heels of his new cowboy boots over one of the rails and watched the proceedings below.

This was luck, to run into such an exciting project his very first day. There was a round central corral and from it were several smaller corrals, some containing small calves, some holding mothers and calves. A few calves at a time were hazed into the large corral. Several cowboys on horseback rode slowly about with swinging ropes. Suddenly one of those ropes would snake out and catch a calf, which would struggle and bawl. Then two men or a man and a boy would hold the calf while someone else slapped a red-hot branding iron on a flank and someone else jabbed the bawling creature with a large hypodermic needle.

Dust was thick and there was the odor of burning flesh and hair and sweat. Dave sniffed it in. This was living! At first he felt sorry for the calves that were being used so roughly, but when they were turned out of the corral, they ran to nurse their mothers or crop the grass, and did not seem to be suffering much.

The hat of one of the youngsters working in the

corral fell off and Dave saw then that the brown hair was curly all over. Why, it was a girl! And younger than he was! Darned if he would sit there on the fence and be merely a spectator in such exciting work. If a girl could help, he could, too. He jumped down into the corral and when the next calf was roped, he was right there grabbing it by the flanks as he had seen the others do and trying to flip it over. This, he discovered, was a harder job than it looked. One of the cowboys shoved him aside with a curt, "Out of the way, kid."

But Dave did not climb back onto his "opery seat." He could at least sit on the animal's head and help hold it down while it was being branded, and this he did until all of the calves had been branded and the irons cooled and hung up in a small shed. Dave was right there helping with this work.

There were about a dozen men and boys engaged in the branding and Dave wondered if all of them worked here on the Rocking B Ranch all of the time.

He followed the others who went to a long bench beside the house and took turns washing up in tin basins, dipping cold water from buckets.

Then he looked about and saw that long planks

had been set out on sawhorses and half-a-dozen women bustled about spreading platters and bowls of food on this rough table.

"Come and get it or we'll throw it out," a lean but sturdy man shouted. He had a weather-burned face, as all of the cowboys did, but Dave instantly recognized him as his uncle Bill although he had never seen him before. The man looked so much like Dave's dad that there was no mistaking the relationship. The same long straight nose, the unruly cowlick of black hair rising from the forehead —these were the marks of the Brandt men and he knew that he himself was a younger, smaller edition of both men. He decided not to make himself known just then but to mingle with the others and see if his uncle would recognize him.

So he got in line, picked up a tin plate and eating tools wrapped in a paper napkin, and filed around the table heaping his plate with roast beef, potatoes, gravy, vegetables, and several kinds of salad. Then he sighed when he came to the pies and cakes, for there was no more room on his plate.

Windy, on the other side of the table, was grinning at him. "You can come back and restock when you get outside of that," he shouted. "That is, if you have any room inside for pie or cake. To see that heap of food, one would think you'd done most of the work here today."

Dave felt his face grow hot as people looked at him. He quickly left the table and went to sit cross-legged under a tree with three cowboys who looked friendly.

CHAPTER II

As Man to Man

FOOD had never tasted better to Dave. But when the edge was off his hunger, a nagging hurt began to stir within him. Why hadn't any members of the family sought him out? They knew he had arrived, since Windy was there, making himself very much in evidence with his loud chatter and hearty cackle at his own jokes.

No doubt Windy had spoken the truth: he, Dave, was unwelcome at the Rocking B Ranch. His father had sent him here to get rid of him. He would be an unwanted nuisance on a busy cattle and horse ranch. He had expected praise because he had pitched in and done his best to help with the branding. But not a word had been said. The cowboys with whom he was eating ignored him and talked about range conditions, the "calf crop" at various spreads, rodeos, and matters about which Dave was ignorant.

Finally, having finished eating, the cowboys unwound their long legs and rose, without touching their hands to the ground, still holding their tin plates. It looked easy. So Dave tried it, and suddenly fell forward with his face in his tin plate.

The cowboys roared with laughter and one of them picked him up.

"Tenderfoot, aren't you?" he asked, but the manner in which he said it was not unkind.

Dave felt his face burning. "I—I tripped," he stammered.

"The first thing a real cowboy has to learn," said the man soberly, "is how to hunker on his haunches to eat. Then he has to learn to stand up gracefully without touching hands to the ground. Takes practice, but it's one of the marks of the true cowboy."

Dave suspected that he was being teased, but he resolved to practice this little skill until he could do it without falling flat on his face.

He followed the three men to the table and took a huge wedge of pumpkin pie and one of gooey chocolate cake. The men scattered to join other groups, leaving Dave to himself. When he had finished his dessert he felt uncomfortably stuffed. Some of the men were saddling horses and riding away. Some got into cars with their families. Others stood in small groups talking. The women bustled around cleaning up the mess and washing the dishes in great pans. Dave put his tin plate and eating tools into one of these pans after carefully wiping them off with his paper napkin, as he had seen the others do.

He wondered if all ranch work was made into a sort of picnic as branding seemed to be.

He gazed around and suddenly was aware that several youngsters were staring at him. They had evidently been talking about him. It made him feel self-conscious but he tried to appear matter-of-fact. Now they were moving toward him, three boys and two girls. One of the girls he recognized as the curly-haired one who had been helping wrastle calves.

One of the boys said, "I reckon you must be our cousin Dave."

"I reckon I must be," Dave said, smiling. "I can tell you're a Brandt. You look like your dad over there. He looks like my dad."

"Why didn't you come over and speak?" the curly-haired girl asked.

Dave shuffled his feet. "I was waiting for someone to come up and speak to me," he said. "You knew I was here."

"Golly!" cried his cousin, whose name was Randy. "How could you expect us to know you in this mob? We know the neighbors who always come to help out at branding. But there's always a bunch of strangers—kids from town who come for the fun—and the eats."

"You're the boy who helped me wrastle calves," said the curly-haired girl who must be his cousin Ginny, said. "I didn't know who you were. But now that I have time to look at you, I see that you're a Brandt all right. The same longish nose —the same rooster-comb front lock of hair. I'm glad I don't have it."

"You sure all do look something alike," another girl spoke up.

"Let's get us all straightened out for you," Ginny continued. "I guess you know by this time that Randy and I are your cousins. This girl is my best friend, Molly Gail. We're almost the same age. Eleven. And these are her brothers, Jim and Bob. Bob and Randy are thirteen. Jim is fourteen.

"That makes me the boss." Jim grinned.

A chorus of derisive hoots greeted this remark.

Ginny went on. "The Gails live just across the road. It makes it awfully handy because the bunch of us are together most of the time. Our folks say they don't know whose kids are whose."

Jim and Bob, both gangling lads in skin-tight blue jeans, grinned and shuffled their feet. Molly smiled at Dave and said, "It's nice to have another kid about our age here. We have lots of fun. Only it would have been better if you'd been another girl. There are already too many boys around."

A chorus of "Ho's!" came from the boys.

Bob put in, "Two girls" is two too many. One more would have been the death of us."

It made Dave feel good to be taken into this crowd, but he didn't know what to think of girls being part of the gang. He didn't have much use for girls. Anyway, not city girls. Maybe ranch girls were different. At least, these two seemed pleasant and friendly. More so, in fact, than did the boys, but Dave guessed this might be because girls were naturally more at ease than boys were.

"Well," Bob finally said, "I reckon we'd better hike for home and get the chores done."

"I reckon so," Jim agreed.

"Yes," Molly chimed in. "I don't feel hungry a bit right now, but the chickens'll be starved. So will the cats, the dogs, the colts, and calves."

The three neighbors left and Dave found himself being stared at by his two cousins.

"I hope you'll like it here," Ginny said. "We wouldn't live anywhere else than on a ranch."

"I saw Dad go in the house," Randy remarked. "Maybe you'd better go in and say hello."

"Mom went in, too," Ginny added. "She's probably in the kitchen. We'll go in that way."

They went through a wide, screened porch and entered what was evidently the heart of the home, the kitchen, as gleaming and modern as had been Dave's own apartment kitchen in Chicago.

"Mom!" Ginny cried. "Here's Dave! He jumped right in and helped wrastle calves as soon as he got here. Then he stood around without letting anyone know who he was."

"Glad to see you, Dave." His aunt was plump and motherly-looking and it was obvious where Ginny got her cheery smile. "It's time we were getting acquainted. My land, you're as tall as Randy. And heavier. And you certainly do look like a Brandt."

"That's on account of because he is a Brandt." Ginny giggled.

"Randy," Aunt Nell said, "take Dave in and introduce him to your father. Ginny, help me put the dishes away." She sighed. "I'm glad that branding is over for this time. It's always so much commotion."

"But so much fun," Ginny added.

Dave followed his cousin to the front of the house and into a small room that was obviously his uncle's office. In it was an old-fashioned roll-top desk with every cubbyhole jammed with papers. There were two large overstuffed leather chairs and a swivel chair where a man sat working. Several tables were piled with livestock magazines. On the walls were pictures of horses and prize-winning cattle. In several of the pictures Ginny or Randy stood proudly at the heads of the animals. Blue or purple ribbons were attached to these pictures.

Dave sniffed the air, which smelled of dust and leather—a definitely male atmosphere. He liked this littered room at once. Obviously it was seldom cleaned or straightened up like the rest of the tidy rooms he had glimpsed as he passed.

"Dad," Randy said, "here's Cousin Dave."

The big brown-skinned man whirled his chair and thrust forth a hand that gripped Dave's until he had a hard time to keep from wincing.

"So you're David's boy," he said. "I'd no idea you'd grown so. But of course I should have known. You're only a year younger than Randy. Sit down. I hope you're going to like it here."

Dave sat on one of the great leather chairs. "I hope so, too," he blurted. Then he felt his face grow hot. He realized this wasn't the thing to say.

His uncle looked rather startled. "What do you mean?" he asked.

"Well—" Dave squirmed on the slick chair—"I didn't mean that the way it sounded. Of course, I'll like it here. But I wonder if you'll like having me."

His uncle Bill's bushy eyebrows came up in another questioning look.

"Is there any reason why we shouldn't like having you?"

"I'll try not to be a nuisance," Dave said. "But W— someone told me that city men were always sending their kids to ranches to get rid of them. And I'm afraid that's about the way it is with me. Fact is, my father told me he was sending me here in the hope that I'd straighten out and get some sense. W— most likely you know that I've been a problem kid at home. So most likely you've been dreading having me. Most likely I could go to some camp."

"Windy's been airing his tonsils again," Bill Brandt exclaimed. "I wish there was some way of gagging him. He talks too much and always says the wrong thing when he does."

"You mustn't pay any attention to him," Randy broke in. "None of us does. He just stays around because there's nowhere else for him to go. He's too old to do much work. So Dad gives him a cabin to live in and his grub for doing a few odd jobs."

Bill Brandt leaned forward and put his hand on Dave's knee. "Listen to me, lad. Yes, we know all about you. The fact that you and your father haven't been getting along too well. That you've not been doing well in school and that the last year you've been getting into nearly-serious scrapes. So that puts the whole thing on a man-to-man basis. We understand each other, don't we?"

Dave nodded, swallowing hard at the stiffness in his throat.

"But," the man went on, "as far as we're concerned, you're starting here from scratch. Whatever happened last year or the year before is water under the bridge. Here in the range country we never ask questions about a man's past. All we're concerned with is what he does now. And here men and boys are judged by what they are, not how much money they or their fathers have."

Dave gulped again.

"And let it be understood," his uncle went on, "that we want you here. We didn't have to take you. You're a Brandt. One of us. And we're glad to have you so long as you carry your share of ranch work. We expect that of everyone."

He reached forward and gripped Dave's shoulder. "You're welcome here, boy. Make no mistake about that."

"Second the motion!" came enthusiastically from Randy's throat.

Dave stood up. "I want to start learning to be a real cowboy right away," he said. "I want to be a top hand."

"That's the right spirit." His uncle smiled at him.

"Come with me," Randy said. "We're going to bunk together. I reckon your gear is still in the jeep. We'll bring it in and stow it away."

The two boys carried the suitcases in and Randy moved his own few clothes to make room for Dave's belongings. Dave felt rather foolish that he had brought so much—two good suits besides the pile of stiff new blue jeans and western shirts that he had bought in Denver.

"Well," Randy said when the things were unpacked, "I reckon we might as well hit the hay. Morning comes awfully quick most times."

"What time do you get up?" Dave asked.

"When the rooster crows. At the crack of dawn," Randy said, yawning.

"Gosh! I've never been up that early."

"You haven't? Well, you'd better start getting used to it. Or you won't get breakfast. And Dad wouldn't like that."

"I'll be up if it kills me," Dave said. For some reason it was of utmost importance that he please and gain the liking of his uncle who had spoken to him "man to man" a few minutes ago. There had seemed to be an instant bond of understanding between them and he truly wanted to make good so that his uncle would admire and respect him.

While they had talked in the cluttered office Dave had been aware of Randy's eying his cowboy boots. Now when he took them off, his cousin reached over and picked one up and stroked the soft leather, the intricate inlaid pattern and fancy stitching.

"What wouldn't I give to own a pair of boots like these," he said dreamily.

Dave looked down at Randy's boots, which were scuffed and hardened and beat up looking.

"My dad had 'em made to order for me," Dave said indifferently.

"Golly!" They must have cost money. I'm saving up for a pair of fancy cowboy boots. But I'll probably be as old as Windy before I get 'em," Randy said longingly.

Suddenly Dave felt guilty about his fancy boots. "We must wear about the same size," he muttered, seizing one of Randy's and thrusting his foot into it. "Sure enough. It's just right. I'll trade you."

"You crazy?" Randy cried, pushing the fancy boot back into Dave's hand. "I wouldn't take a trade like that."

Dave shrugged. "Have you got an old pair?" he asked. "I want to start doing regular cowboy work. These are too fancy. I'd get 'em all mucked up."

"Yeh. I've got a pair you can use to work in," Randy said as he eased himself into bed and pulled the covers up under his nose. "That pair in front of the closet. You're welcome to 'em. See you at the crack of dawn. G'night."

"G'night," Dave said, lying down. He was rather hurt by his cousin's curt manner in not accepting the cowboy boots. Dave had offered them as a token of friendship and it was as though his friendship had been rejected.

CHAPTER III

The Horse Hunt

A TERRIFIC clanging broke into Dave's pleasant dream of riding a wild bucking horse that had thrown every rider in the county. He sat astride the animal, raking its flanks with his spurs, holding his wide hat in one hand while the crowd at the rodeo cheered. He groaned, rolled over, and pulled his pillow up over his head to shut out that discordant clanging that was spoiling the pleasant dream. But finally the horrible noise overpowered the cheers of the crowd.

"What the dickens is that racket?" he said grumpily, sitting up in bed.

He was surprised to find where he was. It was no rodeo arena but instead Randy's room on the Rocking B Ranch. Slowly his senses came into focus.

"That's the signal for breakfast." Randy was half-dressed and grinned at the tousled, grumpy look of his cousin. "Better hustle your bustle. Cookie clangs the iron against the triangle by the door just fifteen minutes before breakfast is put on the table. And the men had better be there. Nobody argues with the cook on a cattle ranch."

"Not even your father?" Dave yawned and reached for his blue jeans.

"Not even my dad. Not even Mom." Randy chuckled. "Everyone tries to keep on the good side of Cookie."

Dave yawned again. "That was the shortest night I ever spent. Seems to me I just got to sleep."

"You'll get used to it," Randy said. "Hurry now."

Still feeling groggy, Dave dressed and followed his cousin to the dining room where a long table stood with benches alongside. Already Dave's aunt and uncle and Ginny were seated as were Windy and two men Dave had seen the afternoon before but hadn't met.

"Squeeze in here next to me." Randy pointed to a seat beside him.

"Men," Uncle Bill said, "meet our new hand, my nephew Dave Brandt."

Six pairs of eyes were raised from their plates and stared unblinkingly at the "new man."

"Dave," his uncle went on, "from left to right meet Windy Jackson, Slim Watkins, our foreman, and Shorty Jones. As you notice we don't wait for anyone at mealtime around here."

The cook came bearing a mountainous stack of pancakes. "People are on time to meals around here," he said curtly, "or they go hungry." He gave Dave a piercing glance that indicated his remark had been directed at him.

Dave gulped but managed to spear several hot cakes with his fork as the platter passed him, followed by sausages and fried potatoes. A large bowl of oatmeal steamed in front of his plate.

He gasped at the amount of food the men were stowing away. He was used to fruit and an egg on toast for breakfast.

"Eat hearty." Randy nudged him with his elbow. "We don't eat again until supper."

So Dave shoveled in the food although he had little appetite for such heavy fare so early in the day.

"Men," Bill Brandt announced, "now that we have the calf branding out of the way, we'll start on the horse roundup as soon as we can get going. Spike and the Gail kids will be here shortly. Spike will boss the Gails and Randy and Ginny. Slim and I will direct the rest of you. You men have all been over this route before. Fan out as you always do and haze the herd toward the Dead

Man Gulch corral. Windy will drive the jeep there with bedrolls and grub. Let's get going." He threw his long legs over the bench and left the room.

"A horse roundup!" Dave said to Randy in a low voice. "Gosh! That sounds like fun. Will your dad let me go?"

Randy looked at him and studied him with an uncertain frown. "I don't know," he said. "You'll have to ask him." He turned to rise from the bench.

"But if Ginny goes," Dave persisted, "he'll surely let me go."

"Molly's going, too," Randy said. "But they've been raised on the range. They're as good at riding and range doings as any boy. They even beat me at some things."

He went outside and Dave tagged at his heels. Dust was rising from one of the corrals. Dave looked through the poles and saw men swinging loops, catching plunging horses, throwing saddles on their backs. He looked around for his uncle and saw him talking to Windy. He hurried over.

"Can't I go along on the horse roundup, Uncle Bill? Please let me."

"Of course not," the man said shortly. "It's dangerous and hard work. After all, you're a city boy, Dave."

Dave's heart sank. "But I can ride!" he cried

out. "I've been taking riding lessons for two years. And if girls can go, why can't I?"

His uncle glanced at him and it seemed that he was about to shake his head impatiently. Then he said, "Don't look at me as if I had struck you, lad. I'm in a hurry. Didn't take time to think how you'd feel about being left behind when all the other kids go. They are experienced—old hands at this sort of thing. You could get hurt or foul things up so that we'd lose a lot of time and we're too rushed for that. But you can ride along on the jeep with Windy."

"I don't want to ride the jeep. I want to ride a horse!" Dave wailed, but his uncle had strode away to talk to the men.

There was Slim, tall, lean, erect, his hat pushed back from his strong-featured face. His calm gray eyes held the look that came to men whose habit it was to stare into far distances. Dave had noticed that there was a power about Slim that was hard to define, but he gave the definite impression of a man who could always be depended upon.

Shorty was stocky and sturdy—solidly built. His round face looked as if he had just gotten a bad sunburn. It always appeared that way. His skin never took on the dried-leather hue that was a characteristic of most cowboys.

Dave stood watching them as they listened to his uncle. With every fiber he envied them. They fitted into his idea of "he men."

His uncle climbed onto his horse and rode through the wide open gate toward the blue hills.

A man rode in from the other direction followed by the three Gail youngsters on lively horses. This was Spike.

"Hi, Dave!" the Gails shouted, looking very happy and excited.

"Hi," Dave responded dully. He walked to the corral. Ginny was already on a horse. Randy was making a loop with his rope, ready to catch his horse.

"Did Dad say you could go?" he asked.

"Yeh." Dave nodded.

"Swell! Want me to catch and saddle you a good horse?"

Dave gulped and nodded. He felt a bit guilty about it, but after all Randy hadn't asked him if his uncle had said he could ride a horse. The matter then was on Randy's shoulders. Anyway, here was the chance to show that he could handle a horse and make good as a cowboy. This, he told his conscience, was an opportunity he couldn't afford to miss.

His heart beat fast as he saw Randy's rope snake

out and settle around the neck of a spotted horse. The animal looked rather lively and Dave had noticed that several of the horses did some spirited bucking when the men first mounted them. His riding lessons at the Cherry Hills Riding Academy hadn't prepared him for riding buckers.

Shorty threw the saddle on the spotted horse and called over his shoulder, "I'd better take the kinks out of this boy for you before you get aboard."

He quickly mounted and Dave was very glad he did for the horse had a number of kinks and bucked wildly for a few rounds of the corral, then his head came up and he seemed quite gentle.

"Whirlwind is okay now," Shorty said as he dismounted and handed Dave the reins. "Range horses generally have to have the kinks removed these cool mornings early in the season."

"Thanks," Dave said, taking the reins and climbing into the saddle with what he hoped was a careless air.

Randy was on his horse. So was Ginny on hers. Dave reined his mount to follow his cousin and then they all with the Gail youngsters followed the foreman, Spike, toward the blue hills.

Dave felt the breeze against his cheeks, sniffed in the air tangy with the smell of sage and crushed grass, felt the strength of the horse between his legs, and a wild feeling of excitement swept through him. This was Living with a capital letter.

He reined his horse close to Randy's and grinned over at him happily.

"I'm sure glad that Dad let you go along," his cousin said. "I was afraid he'd think you too much of a tenderfoot."

Dave kept still, but his smile faded. He decided that it was not necessary to tell that he was supposed to be riding in the jeep. It was too late to do anything about that matter now.

"What do you do on a horse roundup?" he asked by way of changing the subject. "I thought the Rocking B was a cow outfit."

"It is, mainly," Randy shouted. "But Dad has taken over the running of the Lazy G Ranch across the road. That's where the Gail kids live. Their dad died a couple of years ago. He raised mainly horses. The job of running the ranch is too much for their mother so Dad helps out. It's their horses we're rounding up now. We have a big spring roundup of horses just like we do of cows and calves. Too bad you missed that. We bring the horses in. The colts are branded and the best of the two-year-olds are broken and trained for work on cattle ranches. The Lazy G raises mostly quarter horses."

"Quarter horses?" Dave hated to show his ignorance, but he had no idea what a quarter horse was.

"You're riding a quarter horse now," Randy told him. "And a darned good one. They're called that because they can outrun most any other horse for a quarter of a mile, but then their speed gives out. But they have lots of endurance on the range. I'm riding one, too. That's about the only kind they use on working ranches any more. You can see they are kind of stocky—short-bodied, but they can turn on a dime and give you a nickel change. And do they have cow sense! A good cow pony is the most valuable animal on a cattle ranch. They know what a cow is doing before she knows herself. You'll see how cow ponies or cutting horses are trained to work before too long."

"But what do we do today?" Dave jerked on the reins to keep Whirlwind close to his cousin.

"Don't yank the reins that way," Randy said, scowling. "No wonder Whirlwind tosses his head. Our horses all have sensitive mouths. Dad sees to it that their mouths aren't spoiled. Rocking B horses are trained to neck rein. Like this."

He showed how his horse would obey his will by a simple pressure of the reins on either side of the neck.

"That's better." He nodded his approval as Dave followed his example.

"A little farther on," he explained, "we'll fan out. Each rider will ride a different draw—or gully. This spread is full of them. We'll put you in a center draw and one that's easy to follow so you won't get lost. See that outcrop of red rocks over there?" He pointed. "Use that as your landmark. Right under that to the east is Dead Man's Gulch. It makes a natural funnel leading to a big corral. Haze any horse you find in your draw toward that. There's a water hole there and the animals follow it naturally. But use your eyes or the mares and colts will outsmart you."

"What do I do when I spot any horses?" Dave asked.

"Just neck-rein Whirlwind in their direction. He'll know what to do. This is a game to these horses. They love it, just like they love cutting out calves."

"Sounds like fun." Dave chuckled.

"You're not kidding. But hug Whirlwind's sides with your knees when he starts working any horses toward the corral. He'll turn quicker than a wink and you'll find yourself sitting on a cactus."

Dave hugged with his knees. "Like this?" he asked.

Randy nodded. "Come on. Let's get going. The others are ahead of us. You follow that big wide draw and do as I told you. We'll meet at the corral in time for supper. We'll sleep out, you know. Windy has bedrolls in the jeep."

He put heels to his horse and was off, leaving Randy alone to follow the big draw and prove that he had the making of a top hand.

He pounded his heels carefully against Whirlwind's sides. The horse spurted forward and Dave grabbed the saddle horn. He was glad that Randy wasn' there to see him do this, for he was sure it wasn't done by real cowboys.

It made him feel mighty important to be riding this draw by himself, doing a necessary job of the range. He must make good today so that his uncle would let him go on doing such work. He would prove that he was no tenderfoot.

But as the sun crawled higher and it got hotter and hotter, it grew tiresome riding up one gully and down another. His muscles, even his bones, ached and he changed position often to relieve the strain. He hoped that soon he would find a stream. Surely Whirlwind must be tired and thirsty, too.

A real cowboy took good care of his horse—rested and watered him often.

He pulled slightly on the reins—to rest his horse, he told himself. The slow pace was easier on his tired muscles. He could have gone to sleep without much trouble.

Then suddenly he saw a motion on the hillside. At first he thought of Indians. Then he had to laugh at himself. Of course there were no Indians here now, although this had once been their hunting ground. It was the swishing of a horse's tail he had seen.

He grasped the reins tight and pulled up Whirlwind's head and reined him up the hill. There was a snort and three horses and two colts went scrambling up the steep side. Whirlwind was a match for them. It was as Randy had said. He was quick in responding to the rein and skillfully headed off the mares and their colts and soon had them running along the bottoms of the gully.

Dave forgot that he was tired. He was driving horses toward the corral. He was making good.

Then, suddenly, a lone mare broke from the others and went dashing up the hillside. Whirlwind turned fast as a flash. Dave hadn't been paying attention—hadn't been gripping with his knees.

In a split second he found himself sitting on the ground. He was not in the middle of a cactus, because there was no cactus here. But there were hard rocks. And he hurt where he had landed. Slowly he rose, testing himself to see if there were any broken bones. He was all in one piece—but a bruised piece. He rubbed himself and stared up the hill in the direction where Whirlwind had gone. He could hear the other horses still running up the gully. And there Dave stood by himself, wondering what to do next.

CHAPTER IV

The Battle of the Stallions

"HI HO, WHIRLWIND!" Dave shouted. But there was no reply except the echo bringing his own words back to him.

The horses had all disappeared and the sound of the clatter of their hoofs on the rocks had died down, leaving nothing but vast, utter silence.

They had been traveling fast, but it amazed Dave that they could have got out of sight and sound with such speed.

He kicked at a rock in front of him. He noticed the curled-up toe of Randy's old boot that he wore. He wished that he had on his own glove-soft custommade boots. He would hate to get them scuffed up on rocks and weeds, but they would be more comfortable than these stiff, heavy things he now wore. He hadn't trudged far until he realized that cowboy boots were never made for walking. The narrow pointed heels were all very well for hooking the feet in the stirrups, but they seemed to come right in the center of the instep. Nevertheless, he managed to scramble to the top of the draw so that he could look about for Whirlwind or the other riders.

When he reached the top, he was able to see for miles in every direction, but there was no living creature save a hawk wheeling overhead.

He cupped his hands to his mouth and yelled, "Hi, ho!" But now there was not even an answering echo.

What bleak, desolate country! This morning, when he was astride a fine horse, he had felt like a king surveying a beautiful kingdom, but now there was nothing but gray earth, gray sagebrush, and a faded sky. He felt as though he were the only living person in a vast, empty world.

He looked around for the outcropping of red rocks that Randy had told him to use as a landmark. But they were nowhere in sight.

"The earth couldn't swallow them up," he said aloud, and started and looked around at the sound of his own voice.

He pushed his hat back from his perspiring forehead. "I reckon I'm lost." He again spoke aloud, taking small comfort in the sound of his words. "But good! Where do I go from here?"

"I s'pose if I find a high spot some place," he answered himself, "after while they'll come and find me. But I'd like to find some water first. Aren't there any creeks around here?"

No answer came, and he began to plod over the rough ground to a round hillock he saw. This was the highest spot around and if he couldn't see anything or anybody from there, he would go back into the gully and follow it. Randy had told him that it would eventually lead to the horse trap where the riders were all to meet that evening.

"I'll wither and dry up if I don't get water before then," he told himself. "Whew, it's hot!"

When he finally reached the top of the hill, there was more of the world to be seen but he was still alone in its vast emptiness. He sank down on a rock, panting. He stretched his aching feet out and wiggled his toes. He was tempted to pull off his uncomfortable boots, but he was afraid that if he did so his weary feet would puff up so that he wouldn't be able to get them back on.

"What a jam I'm in!" he said. He had to smile at himself for liking the sound of his own voice. "Here I was going to do such a bang-up job of being a real cowboy. Now I've messed things up so that most likely Uncle Bill will keep me shut up in the house. Why can't I ever do right? I hoped that out here things would be different. . . ."

He got his breath. His heart stopped thumping so hard and he stared around in all directions. To the right ran a ridge that fell away on both sides and to the west of it lay a pleasant valley, with green grass. Aspens grew on the hillside and along the bottom ran a line of what he guessed were willows.

"That means a stream!" He stood up and hurried along the ridge looking for an easy way down.

But before he found it he heard a sound that paralyzed him—a shrill trumpeting scream. He had never heard anything like it. He stopped in his tracks and looked in the direction from which it had come. It seemed to be from the other side of the valley where there were a number of giant boulders.

Again came the sound followed by a similar scream, but one shriller than the other. Then there was the thud of pounding hoofs. Dave stepped behind a rock so that he would be out of sight of whatever it was. He hoped that some of his companions might be hazing a horse herd down the valley. But why that terrifying trumpet cry?

Peering out, he saw a herd of horses with colts by their sides. They were mares, then. The mares scattered about the hillside. Then came more of the trumpeting screams and into sight galloped two magnificent creatures, one gleaming chestnut, the other palomino gold.

"Stallions!" Dave exclaimed.

The golden horse seemed to be in pursuit of the chestnut one. Then the leader turned and pranced on hind legs. The golden stallion did likewise. Their forefeet pawed at each other. No doubt they were battling for the leadership of the herd. Dave drew in his breath. What a sight!

Manes and tails were flying and two magnificent beasts fought with bared teeth, forefeet, and hind hoofs. They shook the earth. They grunted and screamed and snapped their teeth against each other's flesh, tearing, grinding, kicking.

The mares and colts nickered nervously.

Oh, it was a glorious but a terrible sight! Dave gritted his teeth and clenched his fists until his nails bit into his palms.

First it seemed that the chestnut was winning, then the golden horse. He didn't know which he wanted to gain the leadership. The chestnut looked larger, more powerful. He was driving the golden horse back against the rocks. Their forefeet were flailing each other's flesh. Then the golden horse whirled and struck out with his heels against the rump of the chestnut and threw him to his side. But in a moment he was up and, with great teeth gleaming and nostrils flaring, he was after the golden horse.

"Oh, Golden Boy, fight! Fight!" Dave cried out. There was no doubt now which horse he wanted to win—the smaller, younger animal.

In the next few minutes there were times when Dave grew sick with watching such brute punishment. How could these animals endure so much? Would they kill each other?

The fight seemed to go on for ages, but the chestnut was obviously growing weary. His move-

ments were not so fast. Then, suddenly, the golden stallion leaped forward, whirled, and those heels flew out time and again, landing against the skull of the chestnut. Each kick made a cracking sound.

The chestnut fell to the ground stunned, but still the kicks thudded against head, ribs, and rump.

Finally Dave jumped to the top of the rock, took off his hat, and waved it, shouting at the top of his voice, "Don't kill him, you crazy horse. You've won. Leave him alone."

The golden horse stood on four feet, his head raised, his ears perked forward, his nose in the direction of Dave's voice.

His trumpeting cry rang out, this time with a note of triumph. He started to gallop along the hillside, rounding up his herd of mares and colts, and shortly drove them off behind the rocks from whence they had come.

Dave sank down upon the boulder where he had stood shouting. He felt weak and faint, as though he had taken part in this battle himself. What a sight! He was glad when he saw the chestnut horse struggle to his feet and walk off into the bushes.

"You'll live to fight again, fellow," Dave cried softly. "I'm glad you weren't killed."

He climbed down from the rock and continued his journey along the ridge. He had forgotten his thirst while the battle was going on, but now he was really suffering. There was certainly water down in the valley where the clumps of willow bushes grew, yet he was afraid to venture down there. He had proved himself to be very much the tenderfoot, still he did have sense enough to know that wild stallions were very dangerous. He had heard it or read it some place. No doubt the Golden King was far away with his herd of mares and colts, but the wounded chestnut stallion was down there somewhere, and probably not in a very pleasant mood.

Dave sighed. He limped along on feet that felt like huge, aching blisters. He simply had to find water, not only to drink but to soak his tortured feet.

"Shucks!" he said. "That stallion will be as afraid of me as I am of him. If I stand up and yell and wave my hat, he'll take off for the tall timber. I hope."

He limped down the hill toward the cool-looking green grass and the promise of water. He kept his eyes alert for the stallion, or any other sign of danger, but the valley was still and peaceful, giving no evidence except the trampled grass and broken bushes of the recent struggle for supremacy of two magnificent creatures.

He pushed his way through the willows and found a clear stream. There he threw himself on his stomach, thrust his face into the cold water, and drank deeply. He sat up with a giant sigh, feeling much refreshed. Then he yanked off his boots and, pulling up his jeans, thrust his burning, aching feet into the water. His toes curled. This was about the most heavenly feeling he had ever experienced. If he only had a sandwich now, he might enjoy this adventure. The gurgling purl of the water soothed his senses. It might not be so bad to be lost in this pleasant place—if he had something to eat.

There must be fish in this stream. If he had a way to catch them and a way to cook them, he would make out well enough.

Finally he drew his feet out of the water. He was cooling off all over. He glanced up at the sky and realized that the sun was setting. It would soon be dark and he was still very much lost! He dried his feet on his bandanna handkerchief and put his socks on, then he thrust his feet once again into the instruments of torture the boots had become. Sighing, he got up.

"All I have to do," he told himself bravely, "is

to follow this stream. It will have to lead to some place."

He knew that this was good reasoning, but with dark coming on he did not especially want to be in this valley which was suddenly growing gloomy and menacing with no sunlight to warm and brighten it. Wild animals probably would be coming to the stream to drink as soon as night fell. He shuddered and suddenly decided that he would feel safer up on the ridge where he had been before. There he could see in all directions, as long as there was any light. He could also be seen by those who no doubt were looking for him now. Perhaps he would loom up against the skyline. Or perhaps they would have a huge fire blazing to guide him. The idea gave him a great deal of comfort.

He stumbled and limped up the hill when suddenly a "whoosh" made him stop in his tracks.

There was a long silence. He ventured two more steps. Again came the "whoosh."

It wasn't a very dangerous-sounding noise and Dave finally parted the shrubbery from whence it came and there he stared into the bright eyes of a wobbly-legged colt, a filly, standing beside a mare stretched out on the ground.

He put his hand as far as possible and gingerly

touched the mare on the rump, expecting her to leap up and perhaps attack him. But there was no motion. And the flesh he touched was cold.

"You poor baby!" Dave cried, reaching out to stroke the colt. A shiver ran through her flesh and her ears jerked back and forth as she turned wide eyes on him.

"You're an orphan, aren't you?" Dave said sympathetically. "And I'm lost. The two of us better pair up and comfort each other."

The colt "whooshed" again slightly, but made no attempt to avoid Dave's neck rubbing. In fact, soon she stopped quivering and leaned against him as if for support.

Dave pulled the filly toward him. "One thing's certain," he said. "I won't leave you out here alone in the cold. I'll stay by you and see that nothing gets you, you poor little thing."

It made him feel quite brave and strong to be the protector of this helpless creature.

He found a place between some sheltering boulders in a clump of quaking aspens. Half-lifting, half-shoving the foal, he brought her to this nook.

"Wish I had something to feed you," he said. "Wish I had something to eat myself."

He pulled a handful of grass and offered it to

the little creature. She sniffed the green stuff, but made no attempt to eat. However, she seemed un-afraid of Dave; in fact the little filly clung close to him, nuzzling and snuffing.

Dave settled himself as comfortably as possible between the rocks. It was nearly dark. He man-aged to get the colt to lie down beside him with her head in his lap.

CHAPTER V

Horse Camp

AS IT grew darker, Dave's loneliness of spirit increased. He was grateful for the companionship of the foal. The night rustlings and strange noises were fearsome. The mysterious scramblings through the underbrush might mean the movements of rattlesnakes or some other dangerous creature.

A sudden "Whoo! Whoo!" made him nearly jump out of his skin and the foal snorted with alarm. When the sound continued, Dave laughed at himself.

"Just an old hoot owl," he told the colt, and drew her head to his lap again.

Strange, he thought, how many sounds there were in the night: squeaks, scurryings, and a really terrifying cry that sounded like a soul in torment and a "ya-yap-yurr" which might be the wail of coyotes or dogs—or even wolves!

Then something wet was pushing at his face,

jerking his nose. It all mingled with his dreams at first, then he sat up with a jerk. It was the hungry foal nuzzling at him.

"Hey!" he cried. "I'm not your mother. Poor little thing. Hungry, aren't you?"

The foal jerked back at the sound of his voice, then started her urgent shoving and nuzzling again.

"I wish I knew what to do for you," Dave said, rising and stretching and yawning. He felt sore in every muscle. But it was daylight. The warm sun was shining. The mist was rising from the ground and there was freshness in the air that made a fellow feel glad to be alive, even if he was lost and hungry. Surely he would be found before too long. He might try following the winding stream to some ranch, but what about the orphan who had obviously adopted him?

He put his arms about the leggy creature and said, "Feel strong enough for a long walk this morning?"

It seemed that the colt's legs *were* much stronger, although they still had a tendency to tangle crazily.

"Come on; follow me," Dave said, setting out to walk, but holding a hand down invitingly for the colt to nuzzle.

To Dave's delight, the colt tagged right at his heels and reached out frequently to feel his friendly hand.

"I believe you think I'm your mother." He laughed.

He strode along the ridge overlooking the valley. "I'm so starved I could eat a whole cow raw," he told the colt. "If I could find a cow and had any way to butcher it. But you poor little critter. I wonder if you've ever had a meal. And what happened to your mother, do you suppose? Was she killed by a cougar or a bear? She wasn't bloody, though. Well, I guess you can't tell me. I should have examined her for claw marks or something. Or maybe a hunter shot her by mistake."

As he walked he examined the landscape in every direction for a puff of smoke or cloud of dust. Also what had become of the red rocks that Randy had pointed out as a landmark? Of course, they must still be there. No doubt around the bend of some hill, but now he certainly had no idea where they should be.

"I reckon I'm a tenderfoot for sure," he confided to the colt. "Anyway, I know that my feet really are tender and sore in these darned stiff boots. I wish that Whirlwind horse would show up right now. Believe me, I'll hug with my knees after this."

He heard a faint rattling noise and looked in the direction from which it had come. There was a little haze of dust off to the left. He stood still to watch. Before long over the brow of a hill lurched the jeep.

Dave took off his hat, raised it, and jumped up and down, yelling at the top of his lungs. The colt, alarmed, ran off a short distance, but soon returned.

Evidently Windy, or whoever was driving the jeep, had seen him, for the amazing vehicle clattered over steep embankments and down into the valley and through the stream and up the hill without even pausing for breath.

With a screech of brakes it jerked to a stop beside Dave. Sure enough, it was Windy at the wheel.

"Pesky youngun!" Windy blurted. "A greenhorn always makes a lot of trouble. Lucky you wasn't et up by a mountain lion. I heard one holler last night. What you got there? An orphan. Seems to think you're his ma."

"She really does," Dave said. "I found her in the valley over there. Her mother was lying dead.

I don't know what killed her. But this little filly has really adopted me. And she's more starved than I am."

Windy climbed down and rummaged in the back of the pickup and brought out a can of milk and an opener. He poured some of the milk into a tin cup and diluted it with water from his canteen.

"Got a handkerchief?" he asked.

Dave drew out his, still neatly folded. Windy wrapped several folds of the cloth around his forefinger and wet it in the milk, then he thrust the wrapped finger into the foal's mouth. At first it struggled, then at last it tasted the milk and got the idea and began to suck greedily.

"Hey, now!" Windy protested. "I may need that finger some other time."

It was a lengthy process, and shortly Dave took over the job. After all, he felt that the colt was his—at least until the real ownership had been established.

"Is my uncle very mad at me?" Dave finally asked.

The faded blue eyes looked at him shrewdly. "The boss don't know it yet," he said. "He rode back to the ranch last night. Left us to bring in the herd."

Dave gave a big sigh of relief.

"The rest of us aren't too happy about it, though." Windy punctured his small balloon of assurance. "Here you've wasted a lot of my valuable time. The rest of the kids all fanned out looking for you. You've delayed us getting started driving the horses to the ranch. Means we'll most likely lose a day." He looked up at the sun. "Now there's this pesky animal to tend to. Best thing would be to shoot her. Colts like that won't live anyhow."

Dave quickly threw his arms about the small animal. "Don't you dare shoot her!" he cried. "She's mine! She won't die! I'll take care of her!"

Windy screwed up his withered face, pushed back his hat, and chuckled. "Don't fly off the handle now. It really would be the best thing to shoot the poor little orphan and put her out o' her misery. But I wouldn't have the heart to do it myself. If the boss wants it done, he'll have to get one of the other boys to do the job. But the question is, how'll we get her to the ranch?"

"Can't she ride in the jeep?"

"She might, if you ride in back and hang on to her. Otherwise she might jump out and hurt herself."

"I'll hang on," Dave promised.

It took both of them to lift the struggling animal into the back of the jeep.

"I'll tie her feet," Windy said, doing so.

"Pesky," as he now called the colt, had no liking for riding in jeeps, and Dave could not blame her, for it was as rough a ride as he had ever experienced. But he managed to hang on to keep both himself and Pesky from being jounced out.

"This is worse'n riding a bucking horse," he shouted to Windy, but the noise of the jeep drowned his words.

He was pleased and relieved when they finally reached the camp by the corral. The neatly tied bedrolls lay in a heap beside the ashes of a campfire. Horses milled and neighed in the nearby corral.

Dave jumped down and gingerly wiggled his neck to see if his head was still attached. "All my back teeth are loose," he remarked.

"Oh, that was a smooth ride," Windy said. He loosened the ropes that bound Pesky, and the two of them lifted her to the ground. She ran to the gateway of the corral where she heard the sound of horses.

"Your mama's not there," Dave told her.

He noticed how cleverly the corral had been formed. Actually it was a natural formation of steep cliffs on three sides. A fence concealed by willow brush had been built on the fourth side. Even the great swing gate was covered with brush.

He was standing beside Pesky examining the interesting corral when three shots nearby startled him. He whirled. Windy was lowering a rifle he held in his hands. A slight wisp of smoke rose skyward.

"I was just firing the signal to the other kids that the lost was found," he explained. "Spike, Slim, and Shorty must have gone out to see if they could round up any more horses. We missed a couple of draws last night."

Pesky had lost interest in the sounds and smells of the horses on the other side of the fence and was again shoving and nuzzling Dave.

"That little hoss sure does think you you're her mother." Windy chuckled. "I'll build up a little fire and warm a bit of water to mix with the canned milk. Then you can wet nurse her."

"I haven't had a bite to eat since yesterday morning," Dave blurted.

Windy blinked up at him. "So you haven't," he said. "Well, that being the case, I'll rustle you a bit of grub. There's some biscuits left over from breakfast and you can roast yourself a hunk of beef. And some pork and beans from last night if you aren't too fussy to eat 'em cold.

"I'm not fussy a bit!" Dave cried.

Windy opened up a small cupboard that stood beside the bedrolls. He took out a tin plate and spooned out pork and beans and topped them with three biscuits. It was the most delicious food Dave had ever tasted.

The day wore on. The others did not return. Dave began to be worried. "Do you s'pose something happened?" he finally asked Windy.

The old cowboy shrugged. "I reckon not," he said. "They can all take care of themselves. Not a tenderfoot among 'em." He shot Dave a sly grin. "I expect they ran onto some more horses and will bring 'em in."

"Why don't we get in the jeep and go look for them?" Dave suggested.

"Nope. My roundup days are over, except for driving the jeep and extra odd jobs that come along. Jeeps are mighty handy for going over rough country. But it takes a horse to follow a horse. They can be the dodgingest, contrary creatures when they don't want to get caught."

"I noticed that," Dave said. "That's how come I

got dumped yesterday. I zigged when my horse zagged."

"That's what we all figgered." Windy nodded. "When Whirlwind came in without a rider. But, of course, there's never any telling what fool stunt a greenhorn'll pull."

Dave was getting pretty tired of hearing himself called a greenhorn. "Weren't you ever a greenhorn?" he flared.

"Never was," Windy said, bobbing his chin whiskers emphatically. "I could ride a horse before I could walk. Always had more cow and horse sense than I ever had human sense." He cackled loudly at his own humor which Dave didn't think very funny.

"Looks like Pesky's tired out and wants to take a snooze," he said, motioning his head toward the colt who had laid down in the shade of some aspens. "I think I'll go exploring these rocks."

"Well, don't get lost again. We can't waste any more time looking for you."

Dave promised, "I won't go far."

It was wonderful country for exploring. Great boulders were strewn about as though ancient giants had had a battle here, using them as weapons to throw at each other. There were patches of quaking aspens shivering in the slight-est breeze and stately evergreens pointing sky-ward.

It was easy to imagine this country once the hunting ground of Indians—and no doubt, their battleground, too. In his roaming he startled a round roly-poly creature which darted out of sight between the rocks. He guessed it must be a rock chuck.

Noting a narrow trail leading into a quaking-aspen grove, he followed it and came to a tiny log cabin.

"Whew!" he whistled. "What a swell hideout for a bandit's gang." He must be sure to ask Randy about this place.

He circled it cautiously and peered through the dusty windows. It was dark inside but he could see a plain table and bunk beds against one wall. He tried the door but it was locked.

He left the place to go on with his exploring. Climbing a pile of huge boulders, he saw below him a distinct trail leading to the north. The hidden cabin and this trail leading to nowhere—what could they mean? There seemed to him to be a mystery about them.

Later, being tired from climbing, he sat atop one of the boulders with his hands around his knees and took in the beautiful scene. This would be an ideal place to camp some day. He wondered if his cousins and their neighbors across the road ever went camping. He noticed a motion between the aspens and, peering down, saw that it was a doe with her young fawn. He sat motionless so as not to disturb them. The doe browsed and the fawn tagged and butted her, acting much the way Pesky had acted with him. It was beautiful to watch.

He remembered the scene of the previous day when he had witnessed the battle between the two stallions. He was sure that never in his life would he forget that sight. And here was another one—quite different and much less exciting but just as memorable.

CHAPTER VI

Dave Mothers a Foal

A FARAWAY shouting brought Dave from his pleasant dream world and sent the does and fawn into hiding. He slid down from his boulder and ran in the direction of the corral. Soon the louder shouts and the thud of many hoofs told him that the riders must be returning with a herd of horses. He didn't want to miss the sight of their bringing them in.

He reached the edge of the cliff that formed one side of the corral below. Here he climbed another boulder that would give him a wide range of view.

"Hi yi! Hi yi! Hi yi!" It sounded like a band of Indians. Soon the horse herd came into view, manes and tails flying, heads held high. The riders crowded them close, galloping forward whenever one of the ponies made a dash for freedom. Oh, but it was a pretty sight! Dave's heart beat fast.

Slim was in the lead. "Open the gate!" he shouted. Windy was ready; the great gate swung open and the rider galloped in to haze the horses already captured to the rear of the corral so that they would not try to escape.

The new horses were driven in with Slim directing the operation. Each rider, Dave noted, seemed to know just what to do. Everything moved so smoothly! Soon all of the horses were inside the trap and the riders were outside. The gate swung shut on the trapped animals milling around, stirring up dust. They neighed and snorted. Then one of them let out the same bugle-like call Dave had heard yesterday. He peered through the dust. One horse was beating against the logs of the front of the corral with his forefeet and trumpeting his outrage at this terrible thing that had happened to him.

"Oh, no!" Dave cried out in protest. "Not the Golden King."

But it was—the same palomino he had seen battling so valiantly yesterday. Now the gorgeous creature who seemed created for freedom was penned inside a trap. It was a cruel shame.

Dave scrambled down the hill to where the dusty, tired riders were removing saddles and rubbing down their lathered horses. He went over to Randy, trying not to look self-conscious. "Hi!" he said.

"Hi, yourself," Randy responded, looking Dave over rather coolly. "I see you got found."

"Oh, yes, it's hard to lose a bad penny," Dave said.

Randy went on rubbing his horse with a saddle blanket. Dave wondered if he were angry.

"I had quite an adventure, staying out all alone last night," he said. "Whirlwind dumped me."

"That's what we figured when we saw him come in with reins trailing. It's a wonder he didn't trip on them and break a leg."

Dave couldn't help feeling a bit miffed. Evidently it was more important whether or not a horse tripped and broke a leg than if a boy did. Evidently horses were more important than humans—anyway greenhorn humans—on the Rocking B.

"I didn't make out so bad, though," he went on. "I saw two stallions fighting. Oh, boy! That was the most exciting sight I ever hope to see."

Randy turned to him. "You saw stallions fighting!" he cried. "You're kidding."

"No, I'm not. I really did. A big chestnut fellow and that palomino that's trying to knock the corral gate down right now."

"The luck of the tenderfoot!" Randy said in disgust, giving his horse an unnecessarily rough rub.

"I've lived here all my life and never yet seen wild stallions fight. I'd give my right arm."

"That's not all," Dave went on, enjoying his brief moment of triumph. "I found an orphan colt. Brought her in. Found the mare lying dead. I call the foal Pesky. She's the cutest little thing you ever did see."

But Randy was not impressed. "Too bad about the mare," he said. "I wonder what happened to her. Those orphan colts are generally a nuisance. We usually have to shoot 'em. They almost never pull through unless they have a little age on 'em."

"No one'd better try shooting Pesky," Dave blazed. "She's mine. I found her."

Randy looked at him coldly. "Any livestock found on this range belongs to the Rocking B or the Lazy G," he said. "Of course, some stray stock gets picked up once in a while, but the brand will tell who the owner is."

"Isn't this colt too young to have a brand?" Dave demanded.

Randy nodded. "I reckon so. But the mare most likely had a brand. And it was most likely the Lazy G brand. Did you take the trouble to look for a brand?"

Dave shook his head, feeling more the tenderfoot than ever. "I reckon the colt doesn't really belong to me," he said reasonably. "But out there alone with her last night I got to liking her. I felt as if she was my own."

Just then he felt a moist nose against his hand. Pesky was nuzzling him again. "See what I mean?" he asked.

Randy laughed. "I see," he replied. "Pesky thinks you're her mother. Hey, kids!" he called to the others who stopped caring for their horses and looked up, "Dave's adopted a foal. She thinks he's her mother."

Everyone laughed, and the coolness which Dave had first felt when he spoke to Randy melted. Pesky had helped him out of this awkward situation.

Now that the day's work was over, everyone relaxed.

"I found an abandoned cabin back there in some trees," Dave leaned over and whispered to Randy. "And a mysterious trail leading off across the hills."

"That cabin's a line camp," Randy told him. "A place for cowboys to stop overnight or if the weather gets bad when they're riding the range. That trail must be the short cut to the highway. Sometimes riders use it because it's shorter than from the house, as the crow flies. But in a car it's quicker to take the main road."

"Oh," Dave said, feeling deflated again at having his pretty bubble of mystery pierced.

Then to re-etsablish his sense of importance he went on, "That battle between the stallions was the prettiest sight I ever hope to see. Boy, oh, boy! I'm crazy about horses."

"How about chow, Windy?" Slim asked. "Are you going to let us hard-working horse hunters starve to dcath while you sit around all day?"

"Don't hurry me. Don't hurry me," Windy said, piling twigs to start a fire.

"As if anyone ever could hurry Windy." Jim Gail laughed. "He's the time-takingest man I ever knew."

"Folks that want to eat better hustle in some firewood," Windy announced.

"That means you kids," Slim said, squatting down and pulling off his boots. "My feet are killing me."

Dave wanted to echo this cry, but decided against it, so he stomped around on his aching feet and gathered pieces of wood to lug to the campfire. And Pesky tagged right at his heels to the great delight of all of the gathering.

"You make a darling mother," Ginny teased.

Finally, the fire was going. A great iron pot hung

on a rod over its center. Dave sniffed the smell. Pork and beans again, he said to himself. But he would welcome anything by way of food.

Windy was busy mixing something in a flour sack. Dave moved closer to see what he was doing. It appeared simple. He merely poured some water on top of the flour, added a little salt and baking powder, stirred vigorously with a big spoon, then poured dabs of this mixture into a pan of hot grease on the fire.

"Windy's specialty," Bob Gail nudged Dave and whispered. "Dough dabs, he calls 'em. Claims to have invented 'em."

Before long Windy banged against the iron kettle with his big spoon. "Come and get it before I throw it out," he bellowed.

Everyone lined up, took a tin plate, cup, and eating tools from the back of the jeep and filed by the fire where Windy ladled out pork and beans and canned tomatoes and his dough dabs.

"What you going to do when the pork and beans run out, Windy?" Shorty drawled.

"Got another crate of 'em in the jeep." He shrugged. "And if you don't like the cooking, you know what you can do about it."

"Oh, I love your cooking," Shorty said quickly. "Fact is, I've never tasted biscuits so dainty, so light, so deelish." He tossed one up in the air. "Just look!" he cried. "So light it flew right out of my fingers."

It landed on Jim's bare head. He clapped his hands to his brow and cried, "What you trying to do? Knock my brains out? Bet I'll have a bump big as an ostrich egg."

"Anyone who kicks about the cooking has the privilege of washing the dishes," Windy said, filling his own plate and sitting down cross-legged.

"We all love your cooking!" everyone said in chorus.

"Anything would taste good in the air out like this," Dave put in, trying to be tactful and realizing after the words were out how terrible they sounded.

Windy glared at him. "All right, young man, I've had enough. For that you'll do the dishes. And any more complaints, I resign as cook."

There were no more complaints. And by the time Dave got through washing the dishes, he was determined that from now on he would have only highest praise for anyone who did the cooking.

He expected that some of the others—surely the girls at least—would offer to help. But no one did. Evidently, since he had got himself into this, he could take the consequences.

But while he worked, the other boys went off and dragged in two big logs which were put on the fire. And when it grew dark they all gathered around the campfire and sang western songs. Some of them were familiar enough to Dave so that he could join in. A big round moon sailed high in the sky and there was a good feeling of comradeship. This was the way he had imagined ranch life would be. This was Living.

Everyone laughed when Pesky insisted in crowding into the group to lean against Dave's shoulder. He got up and mixed her some milk and water in a cup and let her suck it from his rolled handkerchief.

"You make such a wonderful mother," Shorty murmured.

The talk drifted to stories about horses. Each of the men had a yarn to tell of some special horse he had owned who "had the world beat." But it was Windy, of course, who topped them all.

"Once I had a mare," he drawled. "She was the smartest horse I've ever seen. And I've seen a lot of 'em. One day I was trailin' cattle over some powerful rough country. Went to sleep and fell off and broke my leg."

Spike snorted. "I s'pose you're about to tell us she lifted you back in the saddle."

Windy shook his head. "Nope. But she did grab hold of my shirt, drag me over in the shade, bring me my canteen—then she galloped off lickety larrup to bring a doctor."

"Does he expect us to believe that?" Dave whispered to Randy.

"But she made one mistake," Windy went on. "She brought back a horse doctor."

This tall tale broke up the storytelling. Everyone rolled up in his or her bedroll with feet to the fire and lay on the ground. The earth made a hard bed for Dave's unaccustomed bones and muscles. But it was more comfortable than that of the previous night had been.

Of course, Pesky lay close beside him with her head across his chest. He stared up at the stars. He did not want to go to sleep right away. He wanted to stay awake and savor the pleasure of the sage-scented air, the comforting crackle of the fire, the feeling of companionship. But the next thing he knew, Windy was banging on the kettle and singing at the top of his rusty voice:

> "Bacon in the pan
> Coffee in the pot;
> Git up and git it;
> Git it while it's hot."

The camp groaned and stirred. Dave sat up, startled, then remembered where he was. He looked around and burst out laughing. Shorty had put on his hat first, then pulled on his jacket. He pulled on his boots last of all.

Everyone stared at Dave.

"Whatcha laughing at?" Randy looked at him in surprise.

"At Shorty. Dressing himself upside down. He started at the top instead of the bottom the way folks do. It just struck me funny."

"That's the way all cowboys do," Randy said, reaching for his hat. "When you pull yourself out of a warm bedroll on a frosty morning, you cover up the barest spots first. That only makes sense."

Dave drew into himself. There he went, showing himself the greenhorn again! Maybe someday he would remember to keep his mouth shut and keep his ignorance from showing.

But Pesky came up, shoved at his face, and made everyone laugh. He soon forgot his discomfort.

Breakfast, as he might have guessed, was pork and beans and Windy's famous dough dabs. Immediately afterward the horses were brought in from where they had been hobbled the night before to graze. They were saddled and there was a great bustle of getting ready to start driving the horses to the ranch corral.

"What about Pesky?" Dave pulled at Randy's sleeve. "I'm not going to leave her."

"Evidently she's not going to leave you either, Mama." Randy laughed. "Don't worry. We'll give you a gentle mare to ride. Most likely Whirlwind would kick Pesky's slats in if you tried to ride him."

"But Pesky won't be able to keep up," Dave wailed.

"You'll be surprised," Randy told him. "There are other colts with the herd, you know. They seem able to keep up almost soon as they're born, seems like. We won't be going so fast that your baby can't keep up. Don't worry. Hey, Shorty, saddle the gentle gray mare for Dave, will you?"

CHAPTER VII

"Take Care of Your Horses First"

THE horses that were to be ridden were all saddled, but Shorty, Spike, Windy, and Slim stood in a small circle holding the reins and arguing about something.

"What's the matter?" Dave asked Randy.

"Oh, they're arguing about how to get the wild stallion to the ranch corral. The rest of the horses won't be too hard to drive. A lot of them have been broken. They'll be plenty lively after having run loose all winter, but they'll soon get trail wise. But that palomino stallion is something else. He's wild and wants his freedom."

"Do you have to take him in? What will you do with him? Seems as if he should be free."

Randy nodded. "It does seem too bad to take these stallions in and break them. It usually takes pretty rough treatment to do it. And it seems like they're meant to be free to roam the prairie. But that way they're a nuisance because they coax the tame mares away to join their herds."

The young people all moved closer to hear the arguing about what to do with the golden stallion.

Shorty wanted to turn him loose. "No one will ever break that animal," he said.

"He's as fine a piece of horseflesh as I ever put eyes on," Spike put in. "I think we ought to try to take him in. Texas ought to be at the ranch any day now. He'll be able to break him. If he can't, that stallion would make a fine rodeo horse."

Slim spoke up in his crisp tone. "We're wasting time arguing. There's no doubt that the stallion is a fine animal. The big question is: shall we try to take him to the home corral or turn him loose? And if we decide to try to take him in, how?"

"Oh, turn him loose!" Dave could not help shouting.

Everybody turned to look at him.

"Want to ride him in?" Windy asked.

Dave realized that he had spoken out of turn.

"You're the foreman," Shorty said to Slim. "It's up to you to decide whether and how."

"Then," Slim said briskly, "let's try to take him in. We'll drive the herd out and get them started on their way and try to hold the stallion back in the corral. Shorty, you and the kids haze the main herd toward the ranch. Windy, you back the jeep up into the corral. Spike and I will put our ropes on the stallion—one around the neck and two over the rump—on both sides. Then we'll tie the ropes to the jeep and haul the stallion in, if he won't finally come willingly."

"He'll tear my Leaping Lena apart," Windy wailed.

But no one paid any attention to him. Everyone got on their horses and seemed to know just what to do. Dave felt foolishly helpless, but he climbed on his horse to be ready to help in any way he saw. Pesky had been tagging his heels and now pushed close to the mare he was riding. "You little fool!" Dave said. "Keep out of the way or you'll get trampled."

The gate was swung open only far enough to let the men riders through one at a time. Dave, Ginny, Bob, Jim, and Molly Gail made a sort of half-circle around the entrance to the corral. They sat tense in their saddles with alert expressions. There was quite a commotion within the corral and Dave wished that he could see what was going on.

Soon the corral gate swung wide open and it was like a flood pouring through. Instantly the young riders went into action, shouting, waving hats, reining their horses expertly. Dave saw the jeep back swiftly through the gate. He heard the stallion trumpet his protests. Then the jeep came forward slowly with the beautiful stallion straining against the rope around his neck, his eyes bulging, his nostrils flaring.

"That's cruel!" Dave shouted. "Let him go. He'll choke to death."

He noticed, however, that Spike on one side and Slim on the other had ropes around the stallion's rump. They hauled on these ropes in such a way as to relieve some of the strain on the neck.

The jeep bounced along slowly. Dave knew that he was expected to do something more than just watch, so he urged his horse forward to help drive the herd of loose horses. And they were loose indeed, at first. It seemed that each horse wanted to go in a different direction, but the riders were quick in getting them bunched.

Dave saw that one mare was taking the lead and the others tended to follow her and the colt beside her. Bob and Jim rode at the front of the herd and guided this mare, and before long the herd was running in a group with only now and then a lone horse trying to break away.

He was proud when he was able to ride out and get one such horse back in the herd.

Pesky would not leave his side. "Why don't you go with the herd?" he asked her. "I've got work to do."

The colt nickered as though in answer.

Dave kept glancing over his shoulder to see what was happening to the Golden King. The jeep crawled along with Slim and Spike riding beside it, looking back to see how the stallion was coming.

"I wish the Golden King could break those ropes," Dave said to himself. "He belongs out here, racing, with his mane and tail blowing. He doesn't belong in a corral or barn and he shouldn't be a rodeo horse."

The sun climbed higher. The drive slowed to a walk as the mares seemingly accepted their fate and followed their leader along the trail.

After several hours Dave's stomach told him that it was about noon, but evidently no stop was to be made. They came to a stream where the horses were allowed to drink, but the riders did not dismount, so Dave did not have the nerve to do so, either, although his muscles screamed for a change.

He looked longingly at the vacant space on the seat in the jeep beside Windy. He had found riding in the jeep almost unendurably rough the previous afternoon; now it looked very tempting to him.

But he gritted his teeth and tried to move around in the saddle to find relief. He had wanted to be a cowboy. No one else was complaining, so he would stick this thing out if it killed him.

As the afternoon wore on, he hurt so much in so many places that he finally grew rather numb.

It relieved his mind to notice that the stallion was no longer fighting the rope around his neck but was following the jeep. Dave rode up alongside Randy and said, "Maybe the palomino back there isn't going to be so hard to tame, after all. He seems to be going along okay now."

"Oh, any horse will do that right soon, if he has any sense at all," Randy explained. "That's the first thing a colt or horse has to learn—the lesson of the rope. If he fights the rope around his neck, he gets chocked. When he eases up, the noose is loosened and he can breathe again. The stallion would be dead by this time if he hadn't stopped fighting the rope around his neck."

"I should think, then," Dave said, "that about all you'd have to do to break a horse would be to rope him a few times."

"That's only part of it," Randy went on. "They learn the lesson of the rope mighty quick. Soon if they feel a rope against the neck, they stop rearing back. But training 'em not to buck with a rider and all of the jillion things a good cow pony has to do takes a lot of training. You'll see how it's done. Dad has hired Texas, the best horse breaker in Wyoming, to come and break the horses for the Rocking B and Lazy G spreads. It's lots of fun to watch. Never a dull moment all summer."

"Could I buy a horse of my own? Train him myself?" Dave asked eagerly.

Randy looked at him thoughtfully. "No reason why you couldn't buy a horse," he said, "if you've got enough money."

"Oh, my dad lets me have about anything I want," Dave cried, but was instantly sorry that he had said it.

"Gosh! I have to earn about everything I get," Randy said. "But I like it that way. Training your own horse, though, is something else. If you've got so much money, you'd better hire a trainer that knows his business."

Dave felt a bit squelched. Had he sounded braggy when he spoke about money? He realized that here on the ranch they had different standards about a lot of things than he was used to.

"Of course, I don't know anything about training a horse," he said. "Or much of anything else on a ranch. But I hope to learn a lot of things. Somehow, training my own horse would make him seem more like my own."

Randy nodded. "That's for sure. I wouldn't take a million dollars for this little Peanuts horse of mine!" He reached forward and stroked the neck of the sorrel he was riding. "I raised him from a colt and gentled and trained him myself. He's smarter than most people."

"Maybe I can buy this little Pesky colt and train her," Dave said hopefully. He was surprised by the scornful look that Randy gave him.

"Do you expect to work a colt that size her first summer?" he asked. "You can't start training them until they're two-year-olds."

"Oh!" Dave felt crestfallen. "She is pretty little."

"Of course, you can keep handling her. Keep her gentle that way," Randy went on. "Dad prefers to gentle his colts rather than break them all at once the way some trainers do. But you can't always do that with range stock."

"Of course not," Dave agreed, although he didn't know really what he was talking about.

They finally reached the huddle of buildings of the Rocking B before sundown. Dave heaved a giant sigh of relief. He had made it—riding all day just like a veteran cowhand and hadn't complained once. Claws of hunger raked at his stomach. He felt that his muscles had all frozen into one position and he hoped that he could dismount without falling flat on his face.

The pony herd was driven into two wide meadows. Dave looked around to see what the fate of the Golden King was going to be. The gate of one of the corrals was opened and the stallion was literally hauled inside, because at the sight of buildings and fences he was fighting the rope again.

The jeep was whirled around and the ropes loosened. And in a few moments Golden King was a prisoner within high fences. Again the wild scream of rage and protest rang out and hoofs pounded the poles.

"That stallion is a long ways from broken yet," Randy said to Dave.

But at that moment Dave was concerned with his own current problem—that of dismounting without making a fool of himself. He hated to admit that his muscles seemed to be paralyzed. He gritted his teeth and made his legs move and shortly he was on the ground and on his feet!

He was about to drop the reins and stumble into the house for a drink of cold water and maybe a handout of food.

"Take the saddle off," Randy told him. "We always take care of our own horses and right away."

Stifling a groan, Dave managed to get the saddle off and thrown over a fence rail, as the others did. Then he saw that he was expected to rub his horse down, then lead him to the water trough, then fork him a meal of hay.

"This is about the longest day I ever knew," Dave whispered to Pesky who was nudging him insistently. "And now, of course, I'm going to have to feed you your warm milk before I get anything to eat myself."

CHAPTER VIII

Dave's Hero Appears

BY THE time he had his horse and Pesky attended to, Dave was so tired that he didn't care whether he ate or not. All he wanted to do was to fall into bed. And most of all he wanted to get his stiff cowboy boots off.

He hobbled toward the house after he had fed Pesky and washed up at the bench beside the porch. The colt poked right at his heels and nudged his elbow while he washed.

"Oh, leave me alone!" Dave sighed. "Run along and bed down somewhere. I'm tired."

He opened the screen and Pesky edged in beside him and ran into the kitchen.

"Of all things!" Mrs. Brandt laughed. "First time I've had a colt in the kitchen, although I've had about everything else."

"I refuse to work here with a colt underfoot." Cooky scowled and put his hands on his hips.

Pesky, though, seemed unaware that she was not welcome. She ran into the dining room where the men were seated at the table. She switched her tail and sniffed, as though enjoying the smell of the steaming food.

Everyone laughed.

"Oh, come on, Pesky," Dave said impatiently, taking the colt around the neck as though to lead her out. But Pesky slipped through his fingers.

"You'll have to go out yourself." Ginny giggled. "Then Pesky'll follow you. She thinks you're her mother. Remember?"

Dave stomped out of the room, feeling not at all amused. In fact, right now he was downright grumpy. He slammed the door almost on Pesky's nose.

Before he returned to the dining room he went to Randy's bedroom and pulled off his torturing boots and put on felt slippers. Right away he was better.

Back in the dining room, he slid onto the bench beside Randy. As the steaming, savory food was passed to him, he was hungry again and piled his plate high.

Windy looked at it and whistled. "The boss isn't going to make any profit off of you!" he exclaimed.

"This looks awfully good," Randy said. "But I'm

sure going to miss your pork and beans and dough dabs."

"Yep," Windy agreed. "It's a special touch I have with food that makes it extra good."

"You must show me how sometime," Cooky, who had come into the room, said sarcastically.

Windy wiggled his chin whiskers and replied. "It's a gift. Not a thing that can be taught."

Dave was almost too tired to finish the last of his cherry pie, but he managed it and carried his dishes to the kitchen, scraped his plate, and put it in the big dishpan on the stove. Then he shuffled off to bed.

"Oh, my!" he sighed as Randy came into the room. "I'm almost too tired to pull off my jeans."

"You've slept in 'em two nights in a row," his cousin remarked. "So it can be done. But not between Mom's clean sheets, I warn you."

So Dave managed to undress and get into his pajamas, and oh, how good the smooth sheets felt when he crawled between them! "Don't wake me up before noon tomorrow," he murmured. "I don't want to go on another horse hunt for a few days."

Randy chuckled. "Okay. I don't think there's anything exciting on for tomorrow."

"I may sleep for a week." Dave yawned.

It seemed that he had scarcely dropped off when

the clanging of the breakfast bell awakened him. And right away people started shouting and moving around. Roosters crowed, hens cackled, horses neighed, cows mooed, dogs barked.

"Grand Central Station would be quiet alongside this place," he said grumpily as he put his feet to the floor and yawned.

Randy was half-dressed. "You'll get used to it," he said. "It's the first hundred days that are the hardest."

"I won't live that long," Dave said. "Not getting along on so little sleep."

"Go back to bed," Randy said. "I'll tell Mom to let you sleep."

"What chance with all this noise going on," Dave growled. Then a grin broke through. "Besides," he went on, "I might miss something."

"You might just do that," Randy said seriously. "There's hardly a day that something interesting doesn't happen. And I think maybe Texas will get here today. You mustn't miss him."

"Who's Texas?"

"The world-famous bronco buster," Randy said. "That's what he modestly calls himself. And he is really good. He can ride the toughest buckers all day with a dollar in the stirrup and never lose a dime."

"Is he going to try to break the palomino stallion we brought in last night?"

"I suppose so. I don't know what Dad's decided to do about him. Come on. Hustle your bustle or you'll miss breakfast. Cooky won't save anything back for slowpokes."

"Cooky really seems to rule this roost," Dave remarked as he buttoned his shirt.

Randy nodded. "Cooks always rule the outfits they work for."

"Are they all as cranky as Cooky?"

"Usually are. Maybe it's eating their own cooking makes 'em that way."

"Cooky's grub is good," Dave remarked. "Today I'm going to wear my tennis shoes. Those boots you gave me about ruined my feet."

"Takes awhile to get used to cowboy boots," Randy said as he went through the door.

After breakfast everyone, including Dave's aunt Ellen, gravitated toward the pasture fence to look over the horses brought in the night before.

As soon as Dave opened the door, he was greeted by an excited whinny of greeting from Pesky.

"Oh, golly Moses!" Dave exclaimed. "I forgot all about you. Now I've got to feed you."

Ginny giggled. "I already fed Pesky. But don't be mad. You can see that she still thinks you're her mother."

Dave wrinkled up his nose at her. "You like to tease, don't you? But thanks for feeding my pest."

"Don't let it be habit forming," she told him. "I just did it out of the goodness of my heart this once. To tell the truth, I didn't expect you to get up at all this morning, you looked so done in last night."

"To tell the truth," he admitted with a grin, "I didn't expect to. But a fellow might as well try to sleep in a boiler factory. Folks and animals sure make a lot of racket around here early in the morning."

He fell in step with her as she went to the fence, and they stood side by side looking at the horses that were now grazing in apparent contentment.

"They don't look very wild," he commented.

"Some of them have already been broken," she said. "Of course they all act pretty wild when they've been out on the range all winter, but they settle down quickly. As soon as Texas comes they'll start breaking the two-year-olds and the wild range stock that joined the herd."

"How about the stallion?" Dave asked.

She shrugged. "Oh, we never know about those. Sometimes they can never be broken."

"Then what happens?"

"Oh, they usually are sold as rodeo horses—or to the glue factory."

"Not Golden King!" he cried in horror.

She looked over at him and giggled. "You sure like that horse, don't you? I don't really think that Golden King will be sold to make glue," she said. "Or horseburger, either."

"Even being a rodeo horse sounds kind of rough for such a handsome fellow."

"Some rodeo horses get to be famous." She shrugged. "And they aren't treated too mean. I really think they enjoy spilling their riders before the grandstands full of people."

"I've never seen a rodeo," Dave said. "Except in the movies. They must be fun."

"Never seen a rodeo!" she cried. "Golly! We have one about every Sunday. Anyway, sort of a rodeo. The cowboys all gather at some ranch and practice roping and riding."

"But that's what they do all week for a living, isn't it?"

"Sure. But they enjoy it so much that they do it on their days off, too, just for the fun of it."

"That's one of the nice things about cowboying," Dave observed. "The men like the work so well that they do it when they don't have to. I wish I lived on a ranch," he added wistfully.

"I wouldn't live anywhere else," Ginny said emphatically.

There was a sudden burst of shouting. "Yi-pee-ai-ay!"

Dave turned in surprise. It was the Gail youngsters running and shouting like wild Indians.

"Texas is here! Texas is here!" they yelled.

"Oh, goody. Texas is here." Ginny stepped down from the fence and jumped up and down with delight.

Randy came over and joined the group. "Fine!" he said with a grin. "Now things will start to happen. There he is now."

Dave looked in the direction the others were staring and saw riding through the gateway a man who personified his idea of a real cowboy. The man was tall and lean and extremely handsome but in a rugged sort of way. He rode a beautiful black horse and sat tall and easy in the saddle as though he were entirely at home on horseback. He wore his wide black Stetson at a jaunty angle. He had on a scarlet shirt and soft green neckerchief. And he wore leather chaps. His saddle was heavily carved and trimmed with silver as was his bridle, and his cowboy boots were even more lavishly trimmed than were Dave's own.

"Wow!" Dave exclaimed in admiration. "He's really rigged out."

Randy nodded. "He can get by with such fancy rigging because he's a rodeo rider. Practically everything he wears he's won at some contest— his saddle, bridle, boots, chaps, belt, and real gold buckle. Even his hat, I bet."

"Texas," Dave said in admiration, "must be quite a guy."

Randy agreed. "You're not kidding. The Circle K, though, down the road has a bronco buster who's almost as good as Texas. They're always having contests."

Texas dismounted and handed the reins of his horse to Shorty. The youngsters gathered around him.

"Hi, sprouts." Texas grinned and Dave felt a warmth, a sort of vitality come from the man. He was forceful.

"Gee!" Dave said to himself, "What a cowboy!"

CHAPTER IX

The Bucking Contest

DAVE knew that he was no expert on the quality of cowboy clothes, but he could see that everything that Texas wore was of the best. His chaps were of soft, fine leather and the gleaming conchas that decorated them were as large as dollars and certainly of sterling silver. But Dave was most impressed by the fact that all of his gear had been won at rodeos—in competition, Randy said, with some of the best rodeo performers in the country.

Texas strode to the fence to look over the horses that had been brought in from the range. Dave had to stretch his legs to keep up with the tall cowboy's long steps. Texas was well over six feet tall, well built, with wide, strong shoulders and narrow hips.

"Good stuff," Texas said after a moment or two.

Dave had pushed himself up so that he was standing on one of the poles of the fence and his

own face was level with that of the bronco buster's.

"I want to buy a horse," he said breathlessly.
"I'm crazy about horses. I want the best horse
there is. Will you help me pick him out?"

Texas turned and smiled at Dave. His brown
eyes were friendly. "Sure enough," he drawled.
"And I know hosses. But who are you? I've never
seen you before, have I? But ah reckon you all
must be kin of the Brandts. You have that look
about your eyes and nose."

Dave nodded. "Bill Brandt's my uncle," he said.
"We all look something alike, I guess—I mean I
reckon."

"What kind of hoss do you want, pardner?"

Dave's heart skipped a beat to have this wonder
man call him "pardner." From that moment he was
Texas' willing slave.

"I want a good horse," he said. "The best."

Texas turned and leaned his arms on the fence
rail. "Depends on what you want to use the hoss
for," he said patiently. "A hoss that'd be best for
roping might not be best for racing—or general
use—or for cutting. A good cutting hoss, to my
notion, can't be beat."

"Is your horse a cutting horse?"

"The best there is. He's also a champion cow-pony. If I wanted to use him in races, I reckon he'd be a winner there, too. But that takes too much out of a hoss. Uses 'em up too fast."

Dave nodded, pretending to understand just what Texas was talking about. "That's the sort of horse I want," he said. "Just like yours."

"Well, sir, there I'm afraid you will have to be disappointed. There isn't another hoss with Midnight's combination of talents in the whole United States."

Randy came up and broke into the conversation. "Come over and take a look at the stallion we brought in yesterday, Tex," he said. "Dad wants to know what you think of him."

Dave stayed right at Texas' heels. It made him feel good just to be near this unusual man. The cowboy climbed up on the poles with Dave on one side and Randy on the other. Ginny, Bob, Jim, and Molly ranged along in a row.

The golden stallion perked up his ears and whinnied shrilly. It wouldn't have surprised Dave to see fire spurt from those flared nostrils.

"Boy, oh, boy!" Texas whistled. "What a beauty!"

"He's a beauty all right," Randy said in a matter-of-fact tone. "But will he ever be any good?"

Texas shrugged. "Maybe not as a work hoss," he

said. "I doubt if you got him young enough ever to train. But wouldn't he make a hit as a rodeo bucker?"

"Oh, no!" Dave cried out. "Not Golden King. He was made to be king of the range."

He couldn't explain what he meant, but making a horse like this into a rodeo bucker was like making a fine artist paint fences. He was rather vague in his own mind, but his instincts protested this use of such a fine animal. At the moment he was disappointed in his new-found hero, Texas.

A voice below called up, "Well, you never can tell what you'll see when you haven't got a gun! Blast my hide, if it isn't Texas. I thought maybe things would be peaceable around here this summer."

Dave gazed down at a rangy-looking man with a beak nose and small, close-set eyes.

"Wal, you spavined old hunk of hoss meat," Texas responded, climbing down and thwacking the stranger resoundingly on the back. "If it isn't Wishbone! Climb up here and look at what the hoss hunters brought in. The kind of range stallion you dream about but seldom see."

"He's a beaut," Wishbone agreed after he had hoisted himself up the top of the pole corral.

Texas and Wishbone looked at each other for

a moment, then grins broke out on the faces of both at the same time. Evidently they had the same idea.

"How about it?" Texas drawled. "Tomorrow's Sunday. How about a contest to start topping off this boy? But I want to make sure it'll be worth my valuable time to ride him."

"*Your* valuable time!" Wishbone shouted. "I'm the one who'll ride that boy. And I won't waste my time for peanuts."

Randy laughed. "I reckon the men will see that whoever wins will have his time made worth while. They always have."

"Talk it up!" Wishbone said, climbing down. "I've got to get back to the Circle K. But we'll all be seein' you Sunday afternoon."

When Dave saw the cowboy walk toward his horse, he realized why the man was called Wishbone.

"Why, his legs are wishbone shaped," he cried, nudging Randy.

"Sure," his cousin said. "He's forked a horse so long his legs are warped."

Shorty, who came up in time to hear this description, put in, "Yeh. He's so bowlegged a yearling calf could run between his legs without ruffling a hair."

"You should talk, Shorty," said Spike, who popped up from the opposite side of the corral. "You have to borrow a stepladder to kick a grasshopper on the shins."

"Zat so? Well, for my money that's better than being built like a snake on stilts. You're so skinny you have to stand twice to make a shadow."

Dave snorted with suppressed laughter at these exaggerated yet apt descriptions. Spike was tall and lean, with extremely long legs encased in skintight blue jeans. Always from now on Dave would remember him as the "snake on stilts."

Sunday afternoon was a lively time on the Rocking B. The men from the Circle K and the Lazy G drifted in, as did men from other spreads. They all moved toward the round corral in which Golden King was imprisoned. Everyone wanted to see the fun and climbed to the "opery rail." Dave found himself perched between Randy and Bob Gail.

"Boy, oh, boy!" Bob cried, his hands gripping the top rail in excitement. "This ought to be some show."

"But where is Golden King?" Dave cried. "I thought he was here in the corral."

"Oh, they drove him into that chute," Randy explained. "Hear him? He's trying to knock the place to pieces." He pointed to the heavy gate across the corral from where they were sitting. "Texas and Wishbone want to do it the hard way. Usually they work a horse over a bit before they try to ride. But these boys are going to do it just like they do in rodeos. Each will ride for ten seconds and do it according to rodeo rules."

Dave asked, "What are rodeo rules?"

"Oh, the rider's got to keep spurring his horse on the shoulders, hold the reins with one hand, not grab the saddle horn . . ."

"Texas drew the first ride," Jim leaned across Bob to announce.

"Golly!" Randy cried. "I wouldn't want to be in his boots."

Several cowboys were atop the fence enclosing the chute from which the stallion would be released when the rider was in the saddle. Meantime, there was a great deal of shouting, of snorting, and pounding of hoofs against wood.

"That stallion's apt to knock the chute to pieces," Randy said with a worried frown.

"I don't see how they can saddle a wild horse like that," Dave said.

"It's a real job. But the men have had plenty of experience," Randy explained.

There was a shout across the way. The gate

swung open, revealing the golden horse standing like a statue with Texas astride his back with hat held high in one hand, the other hand gripping the reins.

"Look how he tight-legs the horse," Randy said to Dave. "He leaves the upper part of his body loose and tucks in his chin so his head won't get snapped off."

Then suddenly it seemed to Dave that the golden horse exploded all over the corral. He leaped and he whirled and swapped ends and all but turned somersaults. Certainly no man could stay aboard that leaping, spinning animal.

Finally a pistol popped and two men rode alongside Golden King and grabbed the hackamore and another rode beside and pulled Texas from the saddle to the back of his horse. Then Golden King was driven into a lane that again led to the chute.

Dave saw Wishbone climb up on the fence ready to drop into the saddle as soon as the horse was quieted down enough.

"Wishbone has a big advantage," Bob said. "Texas has Golden King worn down a little but not much. But Wishbone has seen how he bucks— knows what type bucker he is, so he can sort of be prepared."

But when the great stallion once more leaped

into the corral it seemed to Dave that he did things he had not done before and he was bucking harder than ever this time. In fact, Wishbone obviously was about to be sent through the air and he grabbed the saddle horn to hold himself on.

A great roar of laughter went up from all the spectators.

"He grabbed the apple," Randy shouted. "Oh, boy! That makes Texas the winner of this round for sure."

Again two men rode up, caught the hackamore, and another man eased Wishbone onto his horse. Then the stallion was driven through the gate.

"Anybody else want to take a joy ride on this boy?" Texas shouted.

All of the men sitting perched on the fence declined.

"I kind of like the feel of my head attached to my neck," one of them cried.

"Breaking that hunk of meanness is your job," someone else shouted. "I wouldn't take him on for all the cows in Wyoming."

"How many times will they ride him?" Dave asked.

"They'll let him rest awhile now," Randy said. "But they'll try it a time or two more, I reckon."

"Gee, whillikers!" Dave cried. "I should think that'd be awfully hard on a good horse."

"It's not easy on 'em," Randy admitted. "This isn't the way Dad has his good horses broken for special work."

"You mean," Dave cried in horror, "that Golden King isn't a good horse?"

Randy shook his head. "Oh, he's a beauty all right, but Texas and Wishbone both say that he's a natural-born outlaw. He'll probably be a famous rodeo bucker, because that horse has more ways of bucking than any mustang I ever saw. But what I mean is, he'll never be reliable to use for a work horse."

Dave sighed. What a fate for such a handsome animal! He couldn't imagine him as an ordinary work horse, although the way the cowboys talked, a good cow pony was the smartest thing on four legs. And he still couldn't enjoy the idea of the stallion as a rodeo bucker. That would be a cruel thing for a creature who was created for freedom —to be king of the range. And it made a lump come in Dave's throat to learn that Golden King would be used this way week after week, to furnish sport for the cowboys.

Dave saw Texas and Wishbone sitting on the

fence across the corral engaged in serious conversation. Then they broke into loud laughter and
Wishbone slapped Texas on the shoulder.

Soon the contest began again. Meantime the
great horse seemed to have thought up new ways
to unseat his riders. During his fourth ride, Wishbone sailed through the air and landed with a
thud. Instantly the golden horse whirled again
and Dave heard that shrill, trumpeting cry ring
out. The stallion reared and those sharp forefeet
were about to descend on the man on the ground.
Dave screamed. But the cowboys were ready for
just such a thing. A rope snaked out and settled
around the neck of the palomino. Another rope
whirled and caught those menacing forefeet and
the horse was thrown to the ground. Meanwhile,
Wishbone scrambled to his feet and was picked
up by a horseman.

Dave's heart leaped into his throat.

"Boy, oh, boy!" Randy cried. "That was a close
one. That horse is a killer."

Dave saw that his cousin's face was white.

"That's enough for today, boys," Slim's voice
rang out.

"There's no doubt who's the winner." Bob
laughed. "Wishbone didn't come out very well."

"He'll be back next week for another try," Jim

cried. "And that might be Texas' unlucky day. You never can tell."

Everyone climbed down from the fence, laughing and talking about the wildest horse ever.

Wishbone came limping out and said that he had never seen the like. That horse had more tricks than you could shove into a box car. And he switched tricks every ride. There was no way to outguess him.

"Alibis! Alibis!" the men shouted.

"It was like riding a cyclone without a bridle," Wishbone went on.

"Yeh!" Texas gibed. "That boy threw you so high I thought the birds would build a nest in your hair before you landed."

Wishbone stopped rubbing his bruises and straightened up. "Well, I didn't see you doing too well. When that palomino warped his back and swapped ends, there was sure a lot of daylight showing between you and the saddle. And the way you pulled leather I thought sure you'd yank the horn out by the roots."

Texas' eyes narrowed. "Shucks. The way I stuck to the saddle you couldn'ta got me loose with an ax until I was ready to relax."

A great shout of laughter greeted this last remark.

"You relaxed all right," Wishbone jeered. "Looked to me like you couldn't ride anything wilder than a wheelbarrow with a cushion in it."

The men went on exchanging insults. By this time Dave had learned it was the cowboys' method of "kidding." There was nothing mean about their teasing and neither man seemed to be offended at what sometimes sounded to Dave like fighting words.

Finally Wishbone pushed back his hat and mopped his forehead with his bandanna. "I almost worked up a sweat," he panted. "Where's that bucket of ice-cold lemonade that Cooky promised to make?"

"I saw him set a bucket there by the gate." Dave pointed.

The dipper lay on the ground. So did the lid. And close by Pesky snorted and kicked up her heels in a mischievous manner.

Wishbone seized the bucket and held it upside down to show it was empty. He gave a great angry wail. "That dad-ratted colt of yours! She drank every drop of our lemonade. I'll skin her and use her hide to wipe my feet on."

"Oh no, you won't!" Dave sprang to Pesky's side and threw his arms around her neck.

"Simmer down, Wishbone," Slim laughed. "Cold

lemonade wouldn't be good for you when you're so overheated."

Dave pushed Pesky out into the pasture to get her out of the way. He knew all of the men and boys and girls were thirsty. Probably no one was in a mood to appreciate this latest trick of the colt's but Dave thought it quite clever.

CHAPTER X

A Horse to Ride

SOON after the riding contest was over, the triangle by the kitchen door was clanged. "Come and build your own!" Cooky shouted.

Dave followed the men and boys who lined up to wash at the bench before filing into the kitchen where sliced bread and meat were piled high. It appeared that each man was supposed to "build" his own sandwich. This with hot coffee was the standard Sunday-evening meal, and after the men had made up their Dagwood sandwiches and filled their tin cups with coffee, they went outside to eat on the lawn.

Immediately the talk broke out about the bucking contest, and more insults were hurled back and forth between Texas and Wishbone until Dave was surprised that the men did not get into a fight. The other cowboys also were generous with uncomplimentary remarks. It seemed to be one of the customs of the country. Insults and preposterous bragging were the accepted mode of conversation and no matter what one man said, someone else tried to top him.

It was evident that the attempt to conquer Golden King would go on and on.

"I should think it would ruin a fine horse like Golden King to be treated so rough every Sunday," Dave said resentfully to Randy. His cousin was sitting next to him trying to stretch his mouth open wide enough to bite into a four-inch-thick sandwich.

Randy nodded while he chewed the choking mouthful. Finally he said, "It won't give him a sweet disposition. It'll do one of two things: break him at last or make him into the meanest bucker alive."

"I should think you'd rather see him broken," Dave said.

"No one'll ever break that boy," Bob broke in, "without breaking his spirit."

"A horse with a broken spirit," Jim said, "isn't worth the bullet to shoot him."

Randy agreed. "That's what Dad thinks. He won't have a broken-spirited horse on the place. Bob's right. No one will ever break that stallion's spirit. Jeepers! Does he have talents as a bucker! I never saw the like and I've watched buckers all my life. He pulls new stunts every ride. He'll be more famous than Dynamite, that horse that no one ever rode."

"Is that what you want him to be?" Dave could not keep the shocked tone from his voice.

Randy shrugged. "I don't have any choice in the matter. I didn't make him an outlaw. I reckon he was just born that way like some people are born bad."

Dave put the rest of his sandwich on his paper plate. Somehow the idea of Golden King being either an outlaw or a rodeo horse made him lose his appetite.

The next day the work commenced of breaking and training the horses brought in from the hunt. There was an air of tense excitement and hurry even at breakfast. The men were eager to be at their jobs.

Texas was to break the wildest buckers with Shorty and Spike to help him in the corral.

Bob, Jim and Molly Gail came over with Spike. They were all on horseback and Dave saw that everyone, even the girls, expected to work with horses. Dave tagged at Randy's heels, hoping that he would be allowed to enter into any excitement that developed. But no one paid any attention to him.

They went into a large corral where the work horses had been turned to graze. The Gail youngsters and Spike rode through the gate and with a "Hi, yi!" drove the horses into a bunch. Spike's noose leaped out and caught a horse. Randy quickly lifted a saddle from the fence and threw it on the back of the horse. With a quick motion he was in the saddle. The horse lowered its head and bucked stiffly for a few minutes but did not seem to have much enthusiasm for the job. When it had quieted down, Randy dismounted and let the reins trail. Dave had learned that this was called tying the horse to the ground; most range horses would stay near the place where they were thus "tied."

"Your horse is ready, Ginny," Molly said. "Golly, don't you wish the boys would let us take the kinks out of our own horses in the morning? We could stay aboard as well as they do."

"Yeh," Ginny said, her tone also resentful. "But I reckon they hate to admit that we can do many things as well as they can. Boys!"

She climbed over the gate and went to mount her pony.

"Aren't you going to ride?" Molly asked when she and Dave were standing together.

Dave shrugged. "I hope so. I want to. Maybe Randy will take the kinks out of one of the horses for me. I s'pose he thinks I can't do it myself."

"I bet you could." Molly looked at him approvingly. "I saw you ride and you're good."

It gave Dave a warm feeling to hear her words.

But soon she was given the signal that her horse was ready and Dave was left standing outside the fence looking in. And no one seemed to be doing anything to ready a horse for him to ride. Instead, the riders rode around and around the big corral, galloping, trotting, turning, pulling the horses to sudden standstills, neck reining, and training their mounts in various types of gaits, turns, and stops. Obviously, too, these horses were not inexperienced. He guessed that they had had some training the previous summer and that this was a sort of refresher course to them.

After a while he grew tired of watching this tame performance. "I could do that sort of riding," he said to himself resentfully. "Those kids treat me like the little man who isn't here."

He went over to climb up on the "opery rail" of the corral where Texas was breaking the tough ones. This was more exciting. Windy was sitting there shouting directions. Dave perched beside him.

A big sorrel was let into the corral. He stepped high. His ears perked forward and he turned his head nervously this way and that. Shorty was afoot. His rope swished out and settled over the sorrel's neck. He and Slim hung onto the end of the rope and dug their heels into the ground, but the horse was pulling them along. With a shout, Windy jumped into the corral and seized the rope and lent his weight and strength to the struggle. The sorrel plunged and jerked, frantic with fear and rage. Dave held his breath. What would happen if the men could not hold the animal?

Finally, though, the men were gaining a bit of control and gradually dragged the horse toward the snubbing post in the center. When the animal was a few yards from the post the men quickly wrapped the rope around it.

The sorrel stopped plunging and planted his feet and pulled back on the rope. Dave saw the effect of this action. The noose tightened, shutting off the air. The horse wheezed painfully, then dropped to the ground.

"You've killed that horse, you crazy fools!" Dave shouted indignantly, but no one seemed to hear him.

Windy leaped forward and sat on the sorrel's head and loosened the noose. The ribs heaved as the horse drew in precious breath. In a moment it had resumed its struggles. Dave saw the men work with swift, deft motions to knot a rope loosely around the neck and shoulders, running it back and under the hind fetlock. The rope was then drawn tight, pulling the hind leg close to the body. Making the knot tight, the men leaped aside and allowed the horse to struggle to his three feet. The noose was taken from his neck and forced into his mouth and the end used to make a half-hitch around the nose, forming a rude hackamore. Dave watched closely to see how it was done. Maybe someday soon he would be allowed to help work the horses if he proved himself an apt pupil.

Slim took the loose end of the rope and pulled the sorrel's head from side to side. The animal quivered in every muscle but did not fight.

Dave remembered that Randy had told him that a horse quickly learned and never forgot the lesson of the rope—that the feel of that rough strand against the neck after the first painful lesson was enough. That first lesson taught that the rope had the power to shut off life-giving air.

After the men had moved about the three-legged horse for a time, smoothing their hands over sides and neck, Slim placed a blindfold over the sorrel's eyes. A wild quiver ran through his muscles. Shorty grabbed both ears and held the sorrel's nose close to his chest. Then a saddle blanket was gently put over the back several times. After this a saddle was put on and quickly cinched. The rope binding the hind leg was loosened and Texas was in the saddle.

The sorrel stood still for a long moment after the men holding him had leaped aside. Then he threw a look over his shoulder to see if there was really something on his back. Immediately things broke loose and the sorrel was all over the corral. He was not the bucker the golden stallion was, but Dave had no desire to be in Texas' place. He did not see how the bronco buster stayed aboard this plunging, leaping, twisting animal. But he stayed until finally the now lathered horse raised his head, the signal of submission.

Slim, now on a horse, rode up beside the sorrel and with his help Texas leaped behind his saddle. The saddle was removed from the sorrel quickly, before he could catch his breath, and he was turned again into the holding corral.

All day Dave watched this sort of thing go on. Every horse was different. Some gave in fairly easily, but the men seemed not to have much regard for such spiritless horseflesh. Others they said were too rough and wild or did not "have the makings" of a good cow pony.

Dave wondered how they could tell.

Some they pronounced "Only good for the glue factory," or "crowbait," or a candidate for someone's rodeo string.

Once, when Windy came up to perch beside him for a breathing spell, Dave asked him, "How do you fellows know whether a horse has the makings of a good cow pony, or crowbait, or a rodeo horse?"

Windy shrugged. "Just plain everyday hoss sense, I reckon," he said. "Some folks are born with it. Some learn it. Some never do. Me, I was born with good hoss sense."

"You're modest, aren't you?" Dave chuckled.

"Just honest," Windy responded.

"I'm tired out from just watching." Dave sighed. "I'm glad I'm not a horse. Or a bronco buster, either."

"Bronc busting is exciting work," Windy said. "Once I was the champion bronc buster of the entire West. Until I got stove up in a rodeo. Now all I can do is pretend the jeep's my bucking hoss. But the feel of it is still in my blood. I just can't help jumping down there and helping when things get rough for the boys. Don't know as they could get along without my help, either."

"Probably couldn't," Dave said kindly. He felt sorry for this broken-down cowboy and bronc buster who, like himself, must be on the edge of things without taking active part. It might be fun merely being a spectator at a rodeo, but when everyone else was doing something exciting, it seemed funny to a fellow not to be taking part. He knew just how Windy must resent being "on the shelf."

Finally this work was over for the day. Dave climbed down from the fence feeling sore, bruised, and weary as though he himself had been riding buckers all day.

He hobbled over to where he could look over and see what the young people were doing. But their work was finished, too, and the riders were lifting their saddles from the horses onto the fence and wiping their faces with their bandanas.

When they finally came through the gate, Dave said to Randy, "I'll bet I could help with that sort of work."

Randy looked at him a trifle coolly, Dave thought. "You've got to know what you're doing when you train horses."

Bob broke in, "But he could haze the calves into the corral when we start doing that work."

Dave gave him a grateful smile. But Randy merely shrugged. Dave decided there was no help from that quarter.

After supper he asked his uncle Bill if he could speak to him privately for a moment.

"Of course. Come into my office," the man said. He led the way.

"Sit down," he said, waving to one of the big upholstered chairs. "What's on your mind?"

"I'd like to rent a horse from you," Dave said seriously.

Uncle Bill looked surprised. "Why do you need a horse?" he asked.

Dave explained. "Of course, I want to buy one soon. My dad told me I could buy one. But I want to look around and find just the right horse. I don't way to buy just any animal."

His uncle nodded understandingly. "You are very wise about that. And I suppose that meantime you want a horse to use while you're looking about."

Dave nodded.

Uncle Bill moved some of the papers on his cluttered desk. "Of course, you want a riding horse," he said. "But I wouldn't think of renting you one. After all, you're my guest. Don't worry about it. I'll see that a gentle horse is put at your disposal, but you'll be expected to care for it yourself."

"I'd want to do that," Dave replied. "But I don't want some old plug to ride. I want a real horse. I want to help the other kids with training the young horses."

Uncle Bill's eyebrows went up. "I wasn't aware that I had any old plugs on the place."

Dave realized that he had said the wrong thing. "I didn't mean that the way it sounded. I meant that I like a horse with some get up and go. After all, I'm an experienced rider, you know."

Uncle Bill nodded. "I have just the horse for you," he said. "The bay called Homer. He has spirit without being mean and he's a good cow pony. You'll have to ask questions and learn how to handle such a horse. I won't have his mouth spoiled. He has one bad habit that you'll have to watch out for, but it won't matter while you're working him close to the buildings."

"What's that?"

"His name is Homer." Uncle Bill smiled. "We call him that because he has homing instincts. Most range horses will stay around the same place if the reins are trailed. We call that tying them to the ground, you know. But Homer won't do that. As soon as the rider is off his back he gets a terrific yen for home and will set out pronto. It doesn't even do to tie the reins to a tree. He'll break loose every time. Otherwise, he's a fine and dependable animal. You may consider him your own to use during your visit—that is, if you treat him right."

"I'll treat him right!" Dave cried. "And I want to buy my own horse as soon as I can. If you'll sell me one."

"We're in business to sell horses. Seen anything yet that appeals to you?"

"Only the golden stallion," Dave replied. "But I reckon that's out of the question."

"I reckon it is, if you want a horse to ride. That palomino stallion is a handsome beast. Too bad he's an outlaw. Not much you can do with such."

Dave stood up. "Thanks a million for letting me use Homer. I'll be good to him."

Dave hurried outside to find Randy to tell him the news that he would be allowed to ride Homer. He saw Randy with Jim and Bob Gail go around the corner of the barn. He broke into a run to catch up with them. When he rounded the corner he saw them enter a shed behind the barn. He had seen this shed before and supposed it contained tools or harnesses or something of the sort. He had puzzled over the strange 𝕌 carefully carved into the face of the door. He guessed this must be a brand.

The door closed behind the three boys. Dave could hear them inside, talking and laughing. He tapped on the door and called out, "Open up, you guys. It's me. Dave."

A sudden silence fell. Randy's laugh broke off in the middle. Not a word was said.

Dave knocked again. The silence continued. It chilled Dave—made him draw up inside. Finally he walked away. He had seen the boys go in there several times but had not thought anything about it.

That night, as the two cousins were getting ready for bed, Dave cleared his throat and said, "Why didn't you answer when I knocked on the door to that shed behind the barn? I saw you go in. Heard you laughing and talking."

Randy, seated on the edge of the bed, reached down to pull off a boot. "These boots get tighter every day. Maybe my feet are getting too big."

"Could be," Dave said coolly. "But you don't have to change the subject on me that way. I asked you a question."

Randy straightened up, his face more flushed than it should have been from stooping over.

"If you must know," he said reluctantly, "it's our clubhouse. We call it our hideout."

"And you don't want me to belong?" Dave knew he shouldn't ask such a question, but the words were wrung from him almost against his will.

"We have rules," Randy said. He was plainly uncomfortable.

"Oh, sure! You have rules. Well, you don't have to slap me in the face to make me know when I'm not wanted." He flung himself into bed and pulled the covers close to his chain.

"Don't be mad," Randy said. "I want you. It's just something. Secret rules. You don't understand."

"Sure, I understand." Dave hated the choked-up sound of his voice that told how hurt he was. The covers were warm, but he felt chilled to the bone. That chilled, unwanted feeling was no new thing to him.

CHAPTER XI

Horse Training

THE next morning at breakfast Uncle Bill said, "Shorty, will you cut out that Homer horse for Dave? Pick out a saddle that will fit him, Dave, I mean. From now on he must learn to saddle his own horse—after someone else ropes him."

"Okay, boss," Shorty said.

Uncle Bill turned to Dave. "You'll do what Slim tells you to," he said. "He's running the colt training operations."

Randy and Ginny looked at him, but Dave couldn't tell whether they were pleased that he was to help them or not. Randy threw him a strange look, but Dave turned his head. He wished he could do something to show his cousin that he was not a greenhorn. He yearned to do something spectacular and heroic—make the others beg him to join their club.

Molly said, "Homer's a good horse. I like him

and he'll be all right for you to use around here where there are good, strong fences to hold him in."

Dave smiled at her. Her sunny friendship warmed him. His aunt Nell looked over at him and said, "You're getting to be just like one of the family."

Dave went out and sat on the fence to watch the men rope the horses which were to be used in the work. Texas came up and stood beside him.

"I'm going to ride and help with the work to-day," Dave proudly told him.

"It won't take long for the green to get rubbed offa you," the man said. "Ah knew the first time ah clapped eyes on you that you all had the makings of a top hand."

"Do you really think so?" Dave cried, eager for more of this sort of talk.

"No doubt at all in my mind," Texas said seriously. "And believe me, I know men and hosses."

Dave was about to burst with pride. So Texas could tell by looking at him that he had the makings of a top hand. Texas certainly should know. At the moment Dave fairly worshiped this man whom he had already picked as his hero.

"I'm going to buy me a horse of my own," Dave said importantly, "just as soon as I find the one I want. Remember, you are going to help me pick him out, Texas."

"Sure enough. I already promised you I'd do that. I'm keeping on the lookout for him. Tell me again just what you want."

"I don't really know. One with spirit. One that can run like the wind. One that will do just what I want him to do. I'd sort of like a one-man horse. One that would come to my whistle."

Texas nodded soberly. If Dave's expectations were out of bounds, he gave no indication of thinking so.

"Do you want a horse that's already broken? One ready to ride as is? Or would you rather finish him off yourself? For instance, like one of those half-broken colts in the pasture?" He nodded to where the colts grazed which the youngsters had been working with the day before.

"I've got a horse I can ride until I get my own," Dave cried, his voice excited. "That Homer horse. How long does it take to finish off a horse?"

"These animals will be ready in a few weeks," Texas said. "They've already been gentled, you know. It's mainly a matter of training now."

"Then I think I'd rather finish off my own. Seems to me he would be more mine than if I bought one someone else had finished."

"You're so right," Texas drawled. "Then, of course, you can take over the whole training of this little rascal here when she gets old enough." He reached down to rub Pesky's nose. "You little fool," he said indulgently. "You're a cute little thing. The only trouble with you is that you don't know you're a colt. You believe you're people." He chuckled.

Dave was grateful that the horse trainer didn't make that worn-out remark about thinking that Dave was his mother.

They turned back to gaze at the young horses.

Texas said, "Let's see how good a judge of horse-flesh you are. Look 'em over and pick out the one you think will be a good all-around hoss."

Dave frowned as he studied the animals. Some of them stopped eating and went tearing after each other, nipping each other's rumps, kicking out with slim heels, snorting and racing.

"That one in the lead." Dave pointed. "Isn't he a lively one, though! Plenty of spirit. And what a beauty. I like that color, too. Sort of a reddish gold."

"Chestnut." Texas nodded. "But don't ever try to pick a horse by the color. It's a nice color, all right. And I'd say you have a genuine knack for picking good hossflesh. That would be my choice,

too. A fine head and neck. Deep chest. Trim legs. Good quarters. Plenty of wind in a chest like that. Well formed. A born leader, too."

"Then you agree that's the horse I should buy?"

"Let's wait. They're coming in this direction. Maybe they'll drink from the trough. You can tell a good hoss by the way it drinks."

"You can?"

Texas nodded.

Sure enough the young animals dashed to the drinking trough and pushed their noses into the water. The chestnut playfully tried to edge the others away and kicked out.

"See the difference in how they drink?" Texas pointed out. "Some of them act afraid to get their faces wet. They only touch their lips to the water. But the little chestnut puts his whole mouth and nose under, leaving only enough room to breathe. That's a sure sign of a good hoss."

"Then," Dave cried, "that's the one I want." Instantly he wanted that particular colt more than he had ever wanted anything in the world.

"You're not making a mistake," Texas said. "But better ask your uncle about it before you get your heart set on the matter. He might have other ideas about that particular colt. I've got to go over and start busting those broncs again."

"Are you going to try to ride Golden King again?" Dave asked.

Texas set his jaw. "Every Sunday until he gives in, until he knows I'm his master. I may half kill him in the attempt. But I'm going to ride that horse."

"I wish he'd never been caught," Dave flung over his shoulder as he hurried toward the house. He wanted to ask his uncle about the chestnut colt before he left the house.

"Uncle Bill," he shouted as he raced through the house. He found his uncle still at work writing letters in his office. "I found the colt I want to buy!" Dave cried. "Could you come and look at him before the kids get him all spooked? I want to make sure that I can buy him and have him for my own."

"Well, I was busy," his uncle said. But he rose from his chair and followed Dave to the fence.

Dave pointed out the lively chestnut who was still romping and racing.

"Very good choice," his uncle said. "Very good indeed."

"Then I can have him? You'll let me buy him?"

"He's for sale," his uncle said. "I see no reason why I shouldn't sell him to you. But he isn't ready to ride yet, you know. He's big enough. But he hasn't been trained for riding."

"But I want to do it myself. I don't want any-one else to touch him!" Dave cried.

His uncle stroked his chin thoughtfully. "I know how you feel," he said. "But it might be as well if you let an expert trainer finish him off."

"I'll watch the others. I'll ask questions. I'll learn how to do it right," Dave cried. "Oh, please let me do it myself."

"I'll let you try," his uncle agreed slowly. "I'll watch and see how you're progressing. I don't want any ruined horses being sold on this place. Of course, we do sell the bad ones to the rodeo strings, but this is a fine colt. Not rodeo material, unless used as a roping or cutting horse. It takes patience and skill and plenty of self-control to train a horse."

"I want him to be all my own," Dave said slowly. "I want to train him myself."

"You go ahead and try then," his uncle replied.

He turned to go back to the house. Randy, Ginny, Molly, Bob, Jim, and Slim all rode slowly into the big corral.

"Hey, Dave!" Randy called out a trifle im-patiently. "Shorty has your horse all saddled.

What're you waiting for? Hustle your bustle. I thought you were wanting to help? We'll let you help haze the calves into this corral when we need them. Shorty'll tell you what to do."

Dave hurried to the other corral and found a pinto ready saddled. "Climb aboard," Shorty invited. "There's work to be done. Time's a-wasting."

So Dave climbed onto the pinto and all day helped drive the calves into the larger corral whenever those on that side shouted that they were ready.

At first it was fun and rather exciting. But as the day wore on it grew to be downright monotonous. Dave yearned to be on the other side where the lively colts were being trained to run after the calves while the riders roped them and threw them to the ground. That sort of work seemed more exciting and useful, but he consoled himself with the fact that he was about to have a horse of his own. He couldn't rope anyway, so he would not have been much help in the other corral. And he could allow his imagination to soar to the time when he was astride his own handsome chestnut, roaming the world.

After the day's work was done, Dave asked

Shorty if the pinto, Homer, was too tired for him to take a ride.

"If you give him a chance to rest up. Take off the saddle so he can roll and graze for a while. You could take off after supper," he said.

"Do you s'pose I'll be able to saddle him myself?" Dave asked.

"I'll come out and show you just how it's done," Shorty offered. "After that you'll be able to do it yourself."

So after supper Shorty and Dave went out and the cowboy showed Dave exactly how to saddle the pinto. Then he removed the saddle and had Dave do it himself.

"Now you're on your own," Shorty said as Dave eased himself into the saddle.

Shorty opened the gate and let the boy on horseback out into the world.

Dave flapped the reins and kicked slightly with his heels and Homer broke into a smooth, easy gallop. Astride this good horse, alone and with vast open space before him, Dave felt every inch a king. He had already experienced the pleasant feeling of authority it gives a person to be on horseback—the feeling that he is spiritually as well as physically above the human on foot. But now this feeling was intensified. Now he was owner of the universe!

He rode toward the chalk buttes that loomed like ancient battlements in the center of the ranch. He determined someday to explore this fascinating spot, for Randy had told him that it had once been the stronghold of Indians when they fought for their hunting grounds.

He rode until night began to fall, then he held the reins slack, giving Homer his head. Sure enough, the pinto promptly turned and trotted toward the ranch buildings. Being alone for this short hour—absolutely on his own—gave Dave a special feeling. Peace and a new sense of self-reliance flooded his being.

CHAPTER XII

A Very Special Horse

"**D**AVE," his Uncle Bill said to him one morning, "you'll have to take that Pesky colt of yours across the road to corral in with the colts at the Lazy G. She's getting to be a nuisance around here. Interferes with the training of the young work stock. Your filly will be better off there. Not so likely to get hurt."

"Okay," Dave said a trifle reluctantly. Pesky was a nuisance all right, always right at this heels, and the little dickens often managed to slip into the corral where the work was going on. Then she would kick up her heels, snort, and tear around, demoralizing the horses that were being trained for work.

Dave set out to walk across to the other ranch. It was no problem to take Pesky there, because she capered right along beside him.

"You're a bad influence," Dave told the filly

fondly, putting his hand on the rippling neck. "So you're going to be put with others your own age. You'll have more fun. But you've got to remember that you're really a colt, not a kid. And I'm not your mother. It's time you started growing up, but please don't stop liking me. In a couple of years you'll be big enough to ride, then we'll have lots of fun together."

Mrs. Gail, whom everyone called Honey, came to the door in response to Dave's knock. As usual, the delicious smell of fresh cookies perfumed the air of her kitchen.

"Uncle Bill said I was to turn Pesky in your pasture with the other little colts," he explained. "Pesky is living up to her name. She interferes with the schooling of the older horses."

Honey Gail gave him her warm smile. "You know where the colt pasture is," she said. "Put Pesky in there. And don't worry about her. I'll keep my eye on her."

"She'll probably miss me a lot," Dave said seriously. "She's never been away from me before. And I don't think she knows yet that she's not people."

"I believe that," Mrs. Gail laughed softly. "But as soon as she's with the other colts she'll begin having so much fun that she'll like being a filly. On your way back, stop in for fresh cookies and milk."

"You won't have to twist my arm to make me do that." Dave laughed.

When he got back to the Rocking B he found that Windy was about to set out for town in the jeep to buy supplies. "Want to go along, Cowboy Dave?" he asked.

Dave shook his head. "No, thanks. I haven't anything to do in Longhorn. But I wish you'd buy me a lot of carrots. I'm about to start training the pony I'm going to buy for my own. I'll get some money for the carrots if you'll wait a jiffy." He ran into the house and came running back with a dollar in his hand.

"All of this?" Windy asked. "It'll buy quite a lot of carrots."

"Shoot the works," Dave said in a lofty manner. "The best is none too good for my horse."

Windy chuckled. "I know just how you feel," he said. "Every real cowboy loves his horse. And I reckon there's no feeling in the world like that of owning your first horse."

Uncle Bill had told Slim and the other youngsters that the chestnut was to be Dave's after he had trained it and no one else was to touch him.

Dave, after considerable study of the matter, had decided to call his horse Prince.

After the workout of the horses that were being trained, Shorty roped Prince and Dave climbed over the fence and went toward him with his carrot offering.

Prince had already learned the lesson of the rope, so he stood as long as he had the noose about his neck, but he snorted and a wicked, wild look came into his eyes as Dave approached.

"Talk to him," Shorty called. "Horses like to be talked to. All the time. And darned if I don't think that they get to understand what you say."

"Easy there, boy," Dave said, slowing his motion. "Easy there, Prince. You're going to be my horse. We're going to be friends. We'll have adventures together. I'm your master. I won't hurt you."

The ears perked up as Dave approached. Prince snorted and turned to a kicking position, but a slight jerk on the noose made him quieter.

"Easy, boy," Dave said with an air of authority in his voice. "No funny business now. We're going to be friends."

He extended the carrot. Prince sniffed and finally accepted the offering.

"Touch him, his nose and neck, but be easy about it," Shorty directed.

Dave extended his hand and rubbed the soft nose and neck. Prince quivered in every limb but stood quietly.

"He needs a good rubdown. His coat's awfully shaggy," Dave said.

Shorty nodded. "About tomorrow you can get the currycomb out and give him a good going over. Get him used to your handling him, then you can start halter-breaking him."

"How long will it be before I can ride him?"

"That depends," Shorty replied. "You can never tell about a young horse. Each one is different. Some don't put up any struggle at all. I wouldn't give you two cents for such a horse. Never be worth a darn. This one has spirit. It might not be too easy. But the more you talk to him—get him used to you—the easier it'll be. And a horse that's gentled easy-like makes a better animal than one that's been rough broke."

Dave resolved that Prince would be gentled "easy-like."

The next morning he was up while the world was still pearl gray and he hurried out to the pasture with a carrot. After a moment he whistled softly. All of the young horses raised their heads, but Dave's heart gave a leap of pleasure when he noticed that Prince's ears flicked more than did the others.

"Come here, Prince boy," he called gently. "Come get your morning carrot."

The colt ignored his invitation. Dave climbed over the fence and walked slowly toward the chestnut. The ears perked forward. The eyes widened. A nervous snort came through the slightly distended nostrils.

Dave walked slowly, the carrot extended. He talked in a soothing voice. There was some sniffing and snorting and a threatening turn of the rear to get in kicking position.

"Listen now, fellow," Dave said in a reasonable but firm tone of voice. "None of your funny business. You know that I'm your friend. You belong to me or will when I have you trained. The sooner you learn that I'm your master and that you have to obey me, the better off you'll be."

The colt turned and rolled back his upper lip, and Dave was sure that Prince grinned at him.

"You're a rascal." Dave chuckled. "But, oh, I like you!"

The colt thrust his head forward and took the carrot, munching on it while Dave rubbed his nose, neck, and rump. A great warmth welled up in

Dave's heart. It was like nothing he had ever felt before. He threw his arm over the smooth brown neck and buried his face in the mane. What a good smell his horse had! He was so happy that he hurt. This was his pony. His very own. Or would be.

The carrot finished, the colt leaped away on stiff legs. Then he glanced back over his shoulder at Dave and stood quivering, his eyes rolling, the whites showing, as though he were frightened. He snorted.

"Oh, you!" Dave laughed. "You're just pretending. You're not scared—of me or anything else."

Then the pony broke into a gallop and raced around and around the corral. Other ponies joined in the fun.

Dave climbed over the fence, calling back, "Have a good time, fellow. This very day school will begin for you. It's time for you to settle down."

Happily Dave hurried back to the ranch house. No one seemed to be stirring. The triangle hanging by the back door caught a gleam from the rising sun. Dave chuckled at a sudden impish idea that seized him. On tiptoe he went to the triangle, lifted it from its nail and, taking the bar used to strike it, he crept close to Cooky's bedroom window. Then he let loose with a terrific beating of bar on triangle.

There was a wild snort, then an angry shout from the bedroom. Dave raced and hung the triangle back in place before Cooky could see who had performed this outrage. Then he tore around the house and slipped in the front door.

He had time to get seated on the edge of the bed and seemed to be tugging on his boots before Randy got fully awake.

"Jeepers!" Randy grumbled. "Seems to me Cooky clanged that darned triangle awfully early this morning. We aren't going on a roundup or anything."

"Seems to me that it's pretty early, too," Dave said in an innocent tone. "But I was awake. Decided to get up. I'm going out to take a look at my new horse. I decided to call him Prince."

Randy sat up yawning and rumpling his already tousled hair. "Say hello for me," he mumbled. "But what's your hurry? The colt won't get away. He'll be there all day."

Dave got out of the room fast. It was all he could do to keep from bursting into laughter over his trick. But he did not go again to the pasture. He went outside where he could hear the pots and pans being clattered with unnecessary violence in the kitchen but right now he wanted to avoid Cooky. So he ran across the road to look into the pasture and see how Pesky was faring. He whistled, and the leggy colt came running, thrusting her nose forward with a wild whinny of greeting.

Dave stroked her nose. "You cute little rascal, you. I wish that Prince liked me as well as you do. But I reckon he will before long. Uncle talked as if he was going to let me keep you. Then I'll have two horses. Golly! The start of a string. I'll really be a cowboy by the time the summer's over, owning my own horses and everything."

Honey looked around the door as he went past. "I thought I heard someone," she said.

"I was just having a little visit with Pesky," he explained. "I don't want her to forget me, so I'm coming to talk to her every day. And I'll bring her carrots."

"Fine!" She smiled. "Now that you're here, you'd better stay and have breakfast with us. We have waffles and honey with sausage."

"Oh boy!" he said. Then uncertainly, "Well, I guess it'll be all right. Randy knows I'm not far away, and Cooky never waits for anyone anyway. Thanks; I'll stay."

Dave could not understand the good feeling he always had when he entered the Gail kitchen. Whenever Honey was around, there was a sense of rightness about everything. He had never known his mother, but when he thought about the feeling he had for Honey, he imagined that was the way a boy felt about his mother. And for some reason he felt closer to Bob, Jim, and Molly than he did to his own cousins. Sometimes he liked to pretend that he was their brother, living in their house. He envied the fine family feeling they had for each other, their jokes, their teasing, which was always in fun—never mean—their chatter and laughter. How nice it would be, he thought now, as he stowed away waffles swimming in butter and honey, to be a member of such a jolly, affectionate family.

How lucky the Gail children were to have such a mother! She was always cheery and never seemed to be cross. Nor was there ever any need for her to be that Dave had noticed. Bob, Jim, and Molly adored her and did everything possible to please her.

It seemed almost as if Honey Gail read his thoughts. She pushed back her plate, leaned on her arms, and smiled across at him.

"It seems as if you belonged here," she said. "I feel as if I've always known you."

"Do you?" he asked in pleased surprise. "That's funny, because I feel that way about you."

"Perhaps it's because you remind me so much of your father."

"My father? Do you know him?"

"Of course. I grew up with him. Went all through school with him until he went away to college. Then to war . . ." Her voice trailed off.

"They were childhood sweethearts," Bob, who had just come in, added with a trace of mischief.

But Honey Gail was not disturbed. "Yes, indeed. We were even sort of engaged, but time and distance drove a wedge between us. Now we're very good friends again. We exchange letters quite often." She said it in a matter-of-fact manner, then arose and started to clear the table.

"I'd better shove off," Dave said. "Thanks for the feed."

"See you later," he added.

On his way back to the Rocking B he had a guilty feeling because he liked Honey Gail better than he did his own aunt Nell. His aunt was a kindly person but always bustling around setting the house to rights, baking countless pies and cakes. But she did these tasks as though they were tasks, not because she loved doing them. Maybe that was it, or was it that the Brandts as a family were rather standoffish? Maybe he was that way, too. But not when he was at the Gails' house.

He sighed, knowing that he should be fonder of his own relatives than he was of their neighbors. Especially Randy. The two of them should really be buddies, but Dave never felt especially close to Randy. And the gap between them seemed to be growing wider merely because Dave had picked Texas to be his hero.

The two boys had argued over this matter again last night when they were in their bedroom.

"Golly, but Texas is a swell guy!" Dave had said. "I never imagined any one man could do so many things so well. He ought to be in movies."

"He sure oughta," Randy agreed.

Dave bristled. "I don't like the way you said that. Don't you like Texas?"

"Sure. He's a good bronc buster. One of the best. A rodeo rider. Great on the showoff stuff. But as a regular, all-around he-man, he doesn't shine beside Slim."

"Slim!" Dave's cry was outraged. "What can *he* do?"

"Everything Tex can do and a lot besides. He could take over any day and completely run this ranch. And he's smart as a treeful of owls. And dependable and honest."

"Most folks are dependable and honest," said Dave, as though scornful of such common virtues.

"Well, I wouldn't depend on or trust Tex any further than I could throw that locoed stallion you're so crazy about."

"You're crazy as popcorn on a hot stove!" Dave kicked off his boots.

"And you can't tell skunks from house cats. You sure don't know how to judge men—or horses. Real bottom in a horse counts more than fancy rigging. Same way with a man."

Dave yawned elaborately. "You bore me," he drawled.

Randy's response to this was to flop on his side and indulge in loud snores.

Today, as a result of last night's quarrel, Randy and Dave had been cool toward each other.

Dave worked with Prince until the iron sounded the signal for the noon meal. Dave was famished and licked his lips at the sight of beautiful lemon pies with fluffy meringue.

He ate sparingly of meat, potatoes, and vegetables. Lemon meringue pie was his favorite. He wanted to be sure to save room. There might be enough for seconds.

He was served last. The others around the table were eating their wedges with obvious enjoyment.

When his piece was placed before him he quickly dug in with his fork. But the fork bounced slightly. He used more force. But the fork would not sink in. It was as though he were sawing away on rubber. Some of the meringue stuck to the fork and rolled back. Then he saw that it *was* rubber. Foam rubber coated with egg yolk and covered with browned egg whites. He ate the meringue quickly, but he felt his face redden at the outburst of laughter.

"Don't you like my pie?" Cooky asked, pretending to look hurt.

"I can't stand lemon pie." Dave tried to grin, but it wasn't much fun being the butt of a joke.

"Maybe you won't be clanging the iron at my window in the middle of the night," he said in Dave's ear.

"I sure won't!" Dave promised. But right away he started working his brain to figure out some other trick to play.

The work of training the horses went on day after day. Dave felt rather put out that he was still nothing but a calf hazer at this job, but he couldn't rope and wasn't experienced in training horses, so he said nothing. The highlight of each day was when he worked with Prince.

He had progressed to the point where he could

saddle and ride the colt around the corral. He was teaching him to respond to the reins on his neck. He planned to train him as a cutting pony, for all of the cowboys had said that a good cutting pony was the finest thing in horseflesh, even superior to a good roping pony. Dave hadn't the slightest doubt in the world that his pony was the smartest thing on four legs and so, naturally, he could be made into a cutting horse.

On one of the Sunday shows at a neighboring ranch he had seen a cutting contest and realized why such horses were so highly prized. All that was necessary was for the rider to indicate by neck reining which calf he wanted cut from the herd. From then on it was up to the horse. The best of them would nose the calf out, then with uncanny skill and wonderful intelligence prevent the calf from returning to the herd. In contests of this sort the rider was forbidden to do anything after he had indicated the calf he wanted cut out. Then he sat with loose reins and let the clever horse do the work.

"Golly," Dave said to Randy as they jogged home side by side. "I'm sure crazy about horses. They're wonderful!"

"A good cutting horse can't be beat."

The other youngsters laughed at Dave for taking such fine care of his pony. Every day Dave curried Prince until he gleamed like satin. A cowboy was expected to take good care of his horses, but no other horse on the Rocking B was groomed to such perfection as was Prince.

"They laugh at me for making such a fuss over you," Dave said one day as he worked. "But there isn't another horse on earth like you. You're special, you are. I'll be glad when I can ride you outside the corral. Then we can set out to see the world. We'll have adventures, we will. And someday I'll take you to a state fair and you'll walk off with all the blue ribbons they have for horses, especially the cutting prize. Because that'll prove that you're the finest kind of horse there is."

Dave had once owned a dog and so had known the depth of love a boy can feel for such an animal, but this love for his horse was like nothing else in his experience. Horses were splendid animals worthy of admiration and respect. And his horse was special. Certainly there was no finer one on earth.

CHAPTER XIII

Escape to Freedom

DAVE was so jittery with excitement one certain Sunday morning that he could scarcely eat his regular breakfast. Later he was to put on an exhibition with Prince to show the training that had been going on over the weeks. On the outcome of this exhibition would depend whether he, Dave, would be allowed to buy the horse for his own.

He was ready early but it was the middle of the morning before Uncle Bill got around to taking time to watch Dave and the horse perform. And with each passing hour, Dave had grown more nervous. At last his uncle stalked over to the corral. Dave was sitting on the fence waiting.

"All right, all right," Uncle Bill said in his brisk way. "Let's get going. I haven't much time. I told Lem Watkins I'd meet him in town this afternoon."

Dave tried to whistle to summon the horse, but his whistle was a dismal failure. He would have liked to have this show a private one, with only his uncle to watch, but of course all of the others came up and took places on the rail. Dave groaned inwardly.

He moved his tongue around inside his mouth to try to "wet his whistle," as his uncle had laughingly told him to do. His second attempt to summon the horse was successful. Prince perked up his ears and came high-stepping toward Dave. He moved his head back and forth, obviously made uneasy by the others perched on the fence.

Dave gave Prince his usual sugar lump and slipped the bridle on, then threw the saddle and blanket across the horse's back. But Prince snorted and jerked and otherwise showed the nervousness that had been passed on to him by Dave and the watchers on the fence.

"Whoa, boy! Whoa, steady now," Dave said, trying to make his voice convey an ease of manner he did not feel. He very well knew that horses could sense the tensions of those around them and that a rider must act self-confident and assured. But right now he, Dave, was neither. His hands shook as he tightened the cinch and he could not hold his voice steady.

But, at last, he managed to get the saddle on and himself into it. He then reined Prince to the opposite side of the corral and rode back and forth there several times in order to steady the nerves of both of them.

"A lot depends upon this." He spoke to the horse in a low, firm tone. "If you want to belong to me, you've got to put on a good show. You've got to let my uncle see that I can handle a good horse. I want you. I want you so much. Don't, please don't spoil it all for us."

As if he understood, Prince threw back his head and shook it until his mane flew. Then he went into the easy, rocking gait that was his natural talent—an easy-to-ride gait which Dave loved and was proud of. Then Dave reined the horse to the center of the corral and round and about time and again in the figure eight, using only reins on the side of the neck for guidance.

He glanced toward his uncle. The man gave a nod of approval. "Very good," he shouted. "Are you ready for some calves?"

Dave raised his hand as the signal to swing the gate open. Bob and Randy drove some yearlings into the corral. True to their nature, they huddled together. Dave reined his horse toward the group and nosed Prince in the direction of the calf he wanted cut out of the bunch. Prince got the idea right away and went at the work as though he enjoyed it. But unfortunately Dave had selected a very agile and sociable calf. He was determined not to be cut off from his kind and showed uncanny ability in getting back.

Finally, rather than make Prince appear worse than he really was, Dave let the first calf go back into the group and selected another one. Prince did somewhat better, but still the calf managed to get back into the bunch. Dave nudged with his knees for another try. This time Prince could not even get the calf cut out. Dave nosed the horse toward another young steer. This time Prince got him cut out and it stayed out but mainly because it was apparently tired. Perhaps it was an animal that had been worked before and had learned the uselessness of resisting a horse and rider. It went to cropping grass and made no attempt to get back to its fellows.

Of course, those on the fence raised a mighty roar of laughter. Dave felt his face grow hot. His uncle motioned for him to ride over. Dave thought he was going to be called down for the poor showing the horse had made, but his uncle said, "Well done, Dave! You've made a very good start in training that horse. I see that he has the makings of a good cutting horse. And as you know, they are the elite of the horse kingdom in the ranch business."

"I thought he did just awful!" Dave exclaimed.

"No, indeed. The calves didn't cooperate too well. These critters have been worked too often. They must be turned to pasture. I can see very well what Prince will be capable of eventually."

"I wanted him to do as good a job as that Boots horse you ride."

His uncle chuckled. "That's expecting too much of a two-year-old. Boots has been trained as a cutting horse for four years. Prince may equal him in time."

"Then you'll let me buy Prince?"

His uncle nodded. "That's what I agreed. I'll keep my promise."

"Wow!" Dave cried. "I'll write today to my dad for the money. The check should be right back."

"I'm sure it will," his uncle said. "And when you write, tell your dad that I'm very pleased with the job you've done in training this horse. You're a fine lad, and your father should be proud of you, as I'm sure he is."

Dave stiffened in the saddle. He turned his face away quickly so that his uncle could not see his tensed face muscles. He put heel to the pony and rode to the opposite side of the corral where he removed the saddle.

"Good boy!" he said. "Uncle Bill thinks you did

all right. He thinks you'll be a fine stock horse, one of the best of the range. And you'll belong to me. You'll be my horse. As soon as you're mine, I'm going to ride around the ranch on you. We'll have adventures together. There are places around here I want to explore. But there isn't much summer left. School will be starting. Darn school, anyway!"

Right after the big noon meal, Dave sat down to write the letter to his father asking for the promised money to buy Prince. It was the longest letter he had ever written to his father or to anyone else, but he had many things to say about the fine animal that would soon be his own.

He would send the letter airmail. Perhaps someone riding in to town this afternoon would take it and mail it. He had the letter in its envelope and was ready to lick the flap when an afterthought caused him to draw it out again and add a P.S. "I could use more allowance money. I have a little filly. An orphan. She adopted me. I've been using all of my allowance money to buy feed for her and I don't have anything left over to buy presents for folks, or even go to the picture show."

He sealed the letter this time. He had no doubts that something extra would be added to his allowance. Money had never been a problem between him and his father. In fact, Dave supposed that his dad had been overly generous with him, giving him too much of everything except that which mattered most! A lump rose in his throat. He went outside.

He could hear the yells and pounding of hoofs from the corral which told that the usual Sunday-afternoon contest was going on. He kicked at a clod of dirt as he walked along the path leading to the road. He felt sick and had no desire to watch the handsome golden stallion goaded into meanness. Why didn't his uncle put a stop to this sort of thing? In fairness, though, he had to admit that his uncle did not pay much attention to the horse breaking. This was a job he left entirely to Texas; his own time and energies were taken up with other matters about the two ranches.

Dave sighed. He didn't know what to do with himself. He wished that Prince were already his so that he could ride out to explore parts of the country that fascinated him. He could ride to town and mail his letter. He yawned. He might even take a nap, but there was this important letter to mail.

He leaned against the fencepost and, fortunately, did not have long to wait. A car was coming toward him, headed for town. He stepped to the edge of the road and waved the letter. The driver stopped. It was Mr. Reynolds from a ranch to the north.

"Will you mail this letter in town for me?" Dave asked.

"Be glad to," Mr. Reynolds said.

"It's terribly important," Dave added.

The man nodded as he took the envelope. "I'll take good care of it."

Dave leaned against the gatepost watching the car grow small in the distance, then he ambled toward the house and sat on the front-door steps and drifted into dreaming about owning Prince and the fun he would have riding him wherever he pleased.

He was aroused from his daydreams by the clop of hoofs. He looked up and saw a large man on a handsome coal-black horse riding up the driveway. He reined up beside Dave.

"Where's the boss?" the man asked.

Dave looked up into a dark face and took an instant dislike to the man. His eyebrows hung over his deep-set eyes like great bushy caterpillars. He had a beak nose, like a hawk's, and his thin lips turned down at one corner. And across one cheek ran a curved red scar. Dave thought that he was a very villainous-looking character, nor did he like the raspy tone of his voice.

"My uncle's most likely in his office in the house if he isn't asleep," Dave said.

"Well, be a good kid and run in and tell him that Bat Cole wants to see him on business."

Not very eagerly Dave rose and went into the house and delivered his message. He followed his uncle outside and perked up his ears when he heard the man say, "I hear you've got an outlaw horse you'd like to get rid of. I might be willing to buy him for my rodeo string if the price isn't too high."

Uncle Bill shrugged. "A couple of bronc busters are having a hassle with him right now in the round corral. I haven't paid much attention myself. Too busy. I leave the horse breaking to Texas. I've taken his word for it that the horse is an outlaw— can't be ridden. If Texas can't ride a horse, I doubt if anyone else can. Too bad. He's as handsome an animal as I ever met."

Dave saw the man lick his lips and there seemed to be a shrewd greediness about the way he did it.

"Go over and take a look at the animal," Uncle Bill went on. "I don't want any outlaws on my spread. In fact, I'd just as soon be rid of him. My best rider risks his neck every Sunday on him and Tex isn't good for much the next day, either."

"Mind if I let my cayuse crop your nice green grass?" the man said, dismounting. "If not, I'll tie his reins to the ground and go over and take a look-see."

Dave watched the man's back. He had powerful, broad shoulders, lean hips, and long legs. He wore his blue jeans low on his hips the way cowboys did. And as the man climbed up to the top rail to watch the show in the round corral, Dave somehow heartily disliked him. He feared the mean-looking man would buy Golden King for a rodeo bucker.

At that moment Windy came around the corner of the house.

"Come here," Dave said. "I want to ask you something."

Windy sat beside Dave. "What's on your mind? Girl trouble?"

"No!" Dave scoffed. "I don't like girls, except Molly and Ginny. And they're like boys. I want to know who that guy is that just climbed the fence. He says he's Bat Cole. Wants to buy the Golden King for his rodeo string."

"Oh, my! I'd hate that," Windy said.

"Why?"

Windy pulled a long spear of grass to chew. "I reckon it's the lot of an outlaw horse to wind up in some rodeo string. Nothing much else to do with 'em. But I've got sort of fond of that golden fellow. Never saw so much spirit. And he's the handsomest thing on four legs. It might be all right for him to be bought into some rodeo string, but not Bat Cole's."

"Why not?"

"Because he's the meanest man in forty-eight states. And he hates hosses. See that scar on his face?"

Dave nodded.

"A horse kicked him. He's hated horses ever since. He thinks up the cruelest things you ever heard of to do to horses, just to keep them mean."

"But surely Uncle Bill won't sell the Golden King to such a horrible man!" Dave cried out in protest.

"I doubt if he knows of Bat's reputation," Windy said.

"Then I'll tell him."

"He wouldn't believe you," Windy scoffed. "He knows you're crazy about horses and how you feel about Pesky, Prince, and Golden King especially.

He'd think you were just trying to keep the horse from being sold."

"Then why don't you tell him?" Dave blazed.

Windy shrugged. "I've often been told I talk too much. But I do have sense enough to mind my own business sometimes. I usually let the boss run his own affairs. And the other boys do, too. Something funny about that golden horse, though. I can't just figger it out."

"What do you mean?"

Windy shrugged. "Oh, nothin', I reckon. Just the breeze blowin' through my chin whiskers again. Just thinkin' out loud. And bein' as how I don't have much to think with, it generally doesn't amount to much but hot air."

He got up and walked over to the corral to watch the riding contest. Dave wished that Windy had finished what he started to say. There was probably more to it than he let on. Windy was suspicious about something. But what?

Soon the riding was over for the day. Men climbed down from the fence. Texas and Wishbone came out of the corral and in a moment Bat Cole moved over with them, making it seem almost like accident. But as soon as they were together, they drew close and talked earnestly and quietly.

Dave walked quickly over to them. "Are you going to buy the Golden King?" he demanded of Bat Cole. "I don't think that'd be a good idea. He's a killer, you know. You wouldn't want riders killed in the rodeo arena before all those people."

The three men broke into loud laughter.

"I do believe he doesn't want me to buy the stallion," Bat said. "Well, sonny, for your information, I'm going to do that very thing. And it's fame I'm offering your favorite horse. Under my teaching he'll be the most famous bucker ever seen in these parts or anywhere else. And believe me, I'm the guy that can turn out the buckers. Ask these men."

Texas put his arm across Dave's shoulder. "Don't feel bad, kid," he said. "It's like Bat said. The Golden King will be famous."

"That man's cruel. Golden King will be hurt. I—I—can't stand it."

Dave had to turn and run into the house then. He didn't want those men to see the working of his face muscles. He was so mad he was in danger of blubbering.

When the people met for the evening picnic supper, Dave learned that all arrangements had been made to sell the golden stallion to Bat Cole for his rodeo string. He would come back in a few days with a strong horse trailer and the check and then the horse would be his.

Dave put down his sandwich. "I'm not hungry. I feel sort of sick," he said as he left the group and hurried to his room.

Late that night, after everyone was asleep, Dave got up and crept out into the night. He opened the gate of the corral in which Golden King was penned and another gate that would release the horse to the country from which he had come.

"Run, Golden King! Run! You're free!" Swish, swish. He waved his white bathrobe.

The stallion seemed to sniff his way to the gate. Then Dave saw in the moonlight the golden form move through.

"The other gate is just ahead of you," Dave called softly. "Keep going."

The golden horse moved in a straight line, and swiftly, but there was no loud thud of hoofs. The stallion seemed to float across the meadow and through the other gate and into wide freedom.

When he disappeared, Dave's spirit soared in a wild leap of happiness. The wonderful stallion was free as the wind. Dave wanted to jump about and whoop and holler. Instead, he tiptoed back into the house and crept silently into his bed.

Later, he awoke. The wind was blowing. Then there was the sudden pounding of heavy rain upon the roof.

He chuckled softly to himself. This downpour would wipe out the stallion's hoofprints, making it harder to follow him.

CHAPTER XIV

The Stallion's Freedom Dearly Bought

DAVE expected a terrible commotion to break forth early the next morning, but things went on as usual. Nothing was said about Golden King. No one noticed that he was gone. Dave drew a sigh of relief, yet he was tense and uneasy. Of course, when the disappearance of the stallion was noticed he would tell of his part, but he hoped that a long enough time would elapse so that the horse could get far away—far enough away so that he would be free forevermore.

The summer days had flashed by like flipped pages in a book. Now it was August. Work on the Rocking B had slackened. Some time each day was spent with the horses, but it was not the intensive job it had been at first. There was more time for play and Dave found that with the boys and girls, as with the cowboys, much of this consisted of the same things they worked at all during the summer. The boys were forever practicing roping.

Dave had tried his hand at this skill and made such a dismal failure that the others had laughed at him, so now he practiced only in private. But he was so poor at it that he grew discouraged and told himself that he didn't want to rope anyway, although he knew that if he ever hoped to wear the title of cowboy he would have to learn to be a good roper. So he made himself go behind the barn and practice whether he wanted to or not.

There was a strong, musky odor in the air. The mother skunk and her four babies were obviously prowling about. Twice he had seen them from a safe distance, the four little ones marching single file behind the mother. It was a pretty and amusing sight.

Now there was time for fishing, a sport that Dave grew to love. And the stream that wandered through the ranch was well stocked with trout. There was a deep pool fine for swimming, where the boys liked to plunge in "raw" whenever they could get away from the ever-present girls. This was often possible now, for Mary Jane, a cousin, was visiting Molly and she was not the tomboy that Molly and Ginny were.

It seemed that all of the ingredients for happiness were at hand, but Dave was not happy, for he did not "belong." The set-apart feeling was more intense now that the work had slackened. Dave went swimming with the other boys, but Jim and Bob Gail and Randy had grown up together and had a great store of shared experiences and a secret code of words which they used to bewilder Dave. And nearly every day the three boys went off to their clubhouse. Dave was never asked to go along, and this fact was building up a store of resentment in his heart.

On the day after he had turned the golden stallion loose, Windy was to drive to town for supplies. Randy was going, too, and asked Dave if he wanted to go along. Usually Dave preferred to stay on the ranch; the small town held no attraction for him. But today he said that he would go. Waiting for someone to discover the disappearance of the stallion was almost more than he could bear.

So he rode Leaping Lena, the jeep, into town. Afterward, he was glad that he did so. It was past the noon hour when they reached town and they went into the hotel restaurant to eat lunch.

While they were eating, a dark-haired woman came over to the table. "Are you David Brandt?" she asked.

Dave nodded, surprised that anyone here should know him.

"I'm the telegraph operator," she explained. "The telegraph office is here in the hotel. A telegram just came for you."

"For me?" Instant alarm seized him. Had something happened to his father?

She smiled. "It's good news," she said. "Strange how most folks think a telegram means bad news. Mostly it's good. Your father wired you a nice sum of money. It will be placed in the bank in your name. All that you have to do is to write a check."

"Boy!" Windy whistled. "I wish I had a dad like that."

"That was quick," Randy said, a trifle enviously. "He couldn't have got your letter until this morning and wow—a check by telegraph."

"Oh, yes," Dave said. "My father's always right there when it comes to money."

Dave didn't mean to have that queer note to creep into his voice, but he could not prevent it. Randy looked at him keenly. "You always act so funny about your father," he said. "What's the matter between you?"

Dave straightened in his chair and he could feel the muscles of his face grow tense.

"Okay! Okay!" Randy said. "Skip it." Then to

the waitress, "I'll have apple pie with a double portion of á la mode."

"Second that order," Dave said, glad to have the subject changed.

Windy shook his head. "The boss will go broke feeding those tapeworms of yours, but long as you've set such a bad example, I'll take the same."

After lunch, and while Windy was buying the supplies, Dave walked into the bank feeling very important. He gave his name and handed the banker the telegram.

"Oh, yes," said the man. "I'm very glad to meet you, David. I know your father. Went to school with him and your uncle."

He handed Dave a pad of blank checks and told him how to fill them out to draw money from his account.

"We're very glad to do business with you," the banker said. Dave couldn't help strutting a bit when he walked from the building.

When they were driving toward the ranch, he couldn't resist pulling out the checkbook so that Randy and Windy could see it.

"Hunh!" Windy said. "I see we're riding with a young oil magnate. It's a wonder you'd condescend to associate with such lowly people as us cow and hoss nurses."

"I have my own bank account," Randy said. "I've earned every cent of it myself. I'm saving it for college."

"Oh!" Dave said, tucking the checkbook back into his pocket. He felt deflated by his cousin's casual remark. Somehow his unearned money seemed not nearly so worthwhile as money one earned himself.

As they neared the ranch, he anxiously reviewed the scene, wondering if the disappearance of the stallion had been noticed yet. But everything seemed peaceful. There was no shouting, no hurrying of riders about on horseback. He guessed that Golden King had not been missed yet. Probably no one paid much attention to him until the Sundays when he was ridden. Water was available in the corral where he was kept and no doubt there was sufficient feed. He had heard Texas say that there was no use wasting good oats on such an outlaw. It might tame him down a bit to starve him for a while.

So Dave sweated out several days waiting for the disappearance to be discovered.

One day during the noon meal his uncle said, "What's the matter with you and that Prince horse? Slim says you haven't been riding him. And

I've been waiting for that check to complete the deal making him your own. I've got the bill of sale ready. Haven't changed your mind about the deal, have you?"

Dave put down the bite of meat he was about to put in his mouth. Suddenly he had no appetite.

"Yes," he said miserably. "Yes, I've decided I don't want Prince. I've—I've decided not to buy him."

"What?" It was like a chorus from everyone around the table.

"Are you crazy?" Randy cried. "You've talked about that horse until I thought you'd die if you didn't get to own him. You worked over him. Made him a one-man horse. No one else can go near him."

"And your father sent you the money," Molly put in, staring at him in amazement.

Dave scowled. "A fellow can change his mind, can't he?"

"Well, I never!" Windy exclaimed. "You do beat all."

Dave was aware that Slim was giving him a strange, half-amused stare. "Maybe the fact that the palomino stallion is gone might have something to do with his decision," he said in his mild tone.

"The palomino stallion gone!" Again the voices shouted in chorus, and each face wore an expression of astonishment.

"This is it," Dave said to himself, putting down his knife and fork and bracing himself to meet the storm.

"The stallion gone!" An angry roar came from Texas' throat. He jumped to his feet and stomped from the room. The door banged behind him and fairly shook the house.

The others were slower to react.

"Are you sure the stallion's gone?" Uncle Bill demanded.

"Positive," Slim said. "I've been making it a habit to look in on him nearly every day. I used to feast my eyes on such a handsome creature. I got to liking him real well. Too bad he's an outlaw. Otherwise, any man would be proud to have him in his string."

Now everyone got up from the table and hurried to the corral where the stallion had been kept.

"I don't understand it," Uncle Bill said after he was certain that the horse was actually gone. "All of the gates are shut. Surely he couldn't have jumped. Not that height. Of course, men have been losing livestock around here lately. There's rumor of stealing. But how could anyone steal an out-law horse?"

Molly put in, "Maybe Bat drove up with his strong horse trailer and loaded the Golden King at night and rode away with him."

"He couldn't load that horse without help," Windy said. "But he might have brought someone along to help. I never did like that guy."

"We haven't any reason to suspect Bat," Uncle Bill said.

"Other than the fact that he wanted that horse very much," Windy said. "And why hasn't he come around to buy him when he was so anxious to get him?"

"That is a point to consider," Uncle Bill admitted, tugging at his chin. "I wonder why he hasn't come back. However, there's nothing to do but notify the sheriff. I'll go in and phone him."

He strode toward the house with Dave tagging miserably at his heels. He followed his uncle into his office and sat on the edge of the big chair.

"There's no need for you to call the sheriff," Dave said. "I let the Golden King out."

Uncle Bill whirled on his swivel chair and set down the phone. "You let the stallion out?" he cried.

Dave nodded.

"Why?" The word came like an explosion. Dave had never seen his uncle so angry.

"Because I didn't want Bat to get him. He's cruel to his horses. And the stallion seemed meant for freedom. I just had to let him go."

"It seems to me you took a great deal upon yourself." The words were cold and icy.

"You were going to sell him anyway. I intend to buy him from you instead of Prince. I've got the check all made out. Windy told me Bat was going to pay two hundred fifty dollars for him."

Dave took the folded check from his pocket and placed it on the desk. His uncle unfolded it and looked at it.

"Well!" he said, and leaned back in his chair as if the strength of his anger had gone from him. "If you haven't got the world beat. I thought you loved that Prince horse so much you had to have him no matter what. Now you turn around and instead buy the stallion's freedom. And now you have no horse of your own."

"I know it," Dave said, twisting his fingers.

"Don't you hate giving up Prince?"

"I hate it more than I've ever hated anything. But I'm not sorry. Somehow it seems more important to me now to save the stallion from Bat. I'm sorry if you're mad at me, but I had to do it."

Uncle Bill drummed on the desk top with his fingertips and seemed lost in thought. Dave could think of nothing else to say. He had made what amends he could by paying for the horse. Now he was ready to take whatever punishment his uncle saw fit. He just wished that they could get it over with.

Finally his uncle ran his fingers through his hair. "You've got me flabbergasted," he said. "You're pretty highhanded for a young sprout. I don't know just what to do about this matter. I'll have to think it over. You run along now."

He picked up the check and placed it in his billfold.

CHAPTER XV

A Skunky Trick

THE days went by and nothing more was said about the freeing of the stallion. But everyone treated Dave with considerable coolness. He wished that his uncle would do something, whatever it was, to punish him and get it over with. This terrible suspense was worse than any punishment he had ever received. And there seemed to be no end to it. He tried to pretend that he didn't care, but he had a feeling that he was overdoing the act; yet he didn't know how else to cope with the uncomfortable situation.

Dave had wondered what Texas' reaction would be to his freeing of the stallion, but the bronco buster had disappeared.

"Where's Texas?" Dave finally asked Windy. "I haven't seen him for a week or so. I saw him ride off one day but I thought he'd be back."

Windy shook his head. "His feet got to itching,"

he explained. "The broncos were busted. It's about time for the rodeo season to begin. That's what Tex lives for. Rodeoin'. It's in his blood for sure."

"I miss him," Dave said.

"We kin get along okay without the likes of that hombre," Windy replied.

"Of course," Dave said tactfully, "he's not as useful around the spread as you are."

Windy's chest swelled. "You just made a very smart remark," he said approvingly. "And just to even the score between us, I'll let you in on a little secret. Something that concerns you."

"What?"

"You're going to have a new ma."

Dave stared at Windy to see if he were teasing, but the old man appeared to be quite serious.

"What are you talking about?" Dave demanded.

"I'm talking about your dad's going to get married."

"How do you know?"

"Oh, I don't miss much that goes on, I can tell you." The chin whiskers bobbed emphatically. "Maybe a little bird told me."

Dave clenched his fists. "Well, either you or your little bird is crazy. I don't believe you."

He turned and ran toward the training corral, for just then he had no heart for doing anything else than watch the beautiful chestnut colt that had almost been his. It gave his heart a wrench to see the animal come high-stepping toward him, his nose thrust out for the expected lump of sugar or piece of apple.

"I'm sorry," Dave said grumpily. "I haven't got anything for you. Run along."

He thought about Windy's bit of news. He had told the old cowboy that he hadn't believed him. But he did. He knew it was true. Suddenly the pieces fitted together. That was one of the reasons his father had been so eager to send him away. A sudden wave of utter loneliness and unhappiness swept over Dave. It was a mood that stayed with him and was not dispelled by the coolness with which he felt everyone was treating him.

He had been wondering lately about school. He had hoped that if things went well he might be allowed to stay here and go to country school with Randy and Ginny and the Gail children. But now the others wouldn't want him. Certainly he didn't want to return to Chicago to live in the same house with the strange woman who would be his step-mother.

What now? Probably he would be sent to some hateful boarding school where he would be as much of a misfit as ever. He heaved a giant sigh.

Now life at the ranch house seemed changed. Ginny spent most of her time across the road with Molly and her guest. Randy, too, quickly disappeared after each meal. Sometimes he and the Gail boys worked with the horses and Dave, pretending to be unconcerned, went on training Prince. Now he was also working a bit with Pesky, halter-breaking her, getting her used to starting and stopping and to having her legs handled. For some reason, it was necessary in horse training to stroke the legs, lift the feet, and pat the rump. It was all part of getting the colt used to his master.

But the happy days he had imagined riding his own horse to explore the interesting places of the ranch had gone glimmering since he did not own a horse. Of course, he considered the golden stallion his since he had bought him, but a lot of good that horse did him. If relations had been less strained between him and his uncle he might have asked him to be allowed to ride Homer on his exploring expeditions, but as matters stood, he dared ask no favors.

So he hung around and tried to keep busy and look perfectly happy, but the old familiar feeling was gnawing away again—the feeling he had known so often. The feeling of not belonging. It had seemed to be different when he first came to

the Rocking B. The other youngsters had acted friendly and he had hoped to be pals with Randy. Then, later, he had grown to feel that his cousin resented him. Actually the Gail boys had acted more friendly than Randy had, but now they had little time for him. In fact, Dave often did not even know where the boys were. Sometimes, though, when he passed the clubhouse he heard them talking or laughing in there and a sick feeling took hold of him.

One afternoon he heard shouting and laughing from the swimming pool and he wandered to the water's edge and stood watching, hoping he would be invited to join the other boys. Finally Bob called, "Why don't you shed your clothes and come in? The water's fine."

A surge of happiness swept through Dave. He quickly stepped out of his clothes behind a bush and dived in and joined in the splashing, racing, and pushing that went on.

Finally Randy said, "Brr, I'm getting cold. I'm going out and warm up in the sun."

"Race you to the other side of the pool and back," Bob challenged Dave.

The race was on. And Dave won. He flashed a smile of triumph over his shoulder, but Jim and Randy were nowhere in sight.

"Probably sunning themselves on a rock," Bob said. "I'll take a look around. You wait here."

Dave swam across the pool and back twice, but Bob had not returned and he could not hear any of the boys. Feeling rather uneasy, he climbed out on the bank and went behind the bush where he had left his clothes. They were gone.

"Those lousy skunks!" Dave cried. "What an ornery trick!"

He crept along the stream behind the bushes as far as he could go. Then he peered out toward the barn. There was no one in sight. He hoped that the girls were safely across the road playing tea party or whatever it was that girls played together. Then he streaked across the open space and into the barn where he picked up a saddle blanket to wrap around himself as he ran to the house.

Fortunately he saw no one although he thought that he heard snickers beside the back porch. He put on fresh clothes and went outside to find the boys to tell them what he thought of them. But they were nowhere in sight. He thought that they were probably in the clubhouse, but pride forbade his going there to find out. It had been made plain to him often enough that boys were allowed inside those sacred walls on invitation only. He had expected to be asked to be a member, but no invitation had been offered.

Windy came bouncing along in the jeep. "I've got to make a hurry-up trip to town to get some supplies from the vet," he said. "Want to go along?"

"I sure do," Dave cried. "I've got important business in town." He climbed up beside the old man.

In town it didn't take him long to go to the feed and grain store and buy a sack of oats and a supply of prepared colt food for Pesky and to the meat market for two pounds of hamburger. When they reached the edge of town on the return trip, Dave asked Windy to stop at the filling station. There was a stand there where fireworks had been sold.

"Got any giant crackers left?" Dave asked the attendant.

"Yeh. I reckon so. Fireworks business wasn't good this year. They don't allow kids to shoot 'em in town any more. I've got some left."

Dave tried to assume an innocent expression as he hurried back to the jeep with his box of giant firecrackers in a sack.

"What's the idea?" Windy looked at him suspiciously. "Fourth of July was a month ago. It's got so it's just another day on the ranch."

"That's why I wanted to make a bang," Dave said in what he hoped was a matter-of-fact manner. "I sort of missed a celebration."

When they reached the ranch he hurried over to the Gail pasture to give Pesky a feast of oats, colt food, and milk. Then he petted her and played with her for a time.

As he was going past the Gail house, Honey called to him, "Fresh cookies and milk now ready!"

"It's nearly suppertime," he said as he entered the cozy kitchen. "But I'm willing to spoil my meal any time for some of your good cookies."

"Flatterer!" She laughed. "I'm glad to have someone eat my cooking. The girls all went visiting."

She placed a plate of warm cookies before him and went on, "Bob and Jim took picnic suppers and said there was an important meeting in the clubhouse. Why don't you take some sandwiches and cookies and join them? I see you just got back from town so naturally you didn't know about this meeting."

The smile faded from Dave's face and it was an effort to swallow the bite of cooky in his mouth.

"I couldn't do that," he said. "You see, I'm not a member. I've never been invited in the clubhouse."

"You've never been in the clubhouse!" she cried in a shocked tone. Her blue eyes snapped. "It amazes me how cruel youngsters can be to each other. I'll see about that. You go over there and tell Bob and Jim to come home this minute."

"Oh, no!" he cried. "They'd hate me for telling. It would make things worse for me. I've got a better plan than that."

"No," she said. "That wouldn't do. I spoke hastily. But why? I can't understand how the boys could be so horrid to you—a guest. I can't understand it. I didn't realize what was going on."

He toyed with the cooky. He felt drawn to confide in this friendly, kind woman. "It's like this," he said, keeping his eyes lowered. "There's something wrong with me. Terribly wrong."

"What on earth can be wrong with you? Are you sick?"

He shook his head. "I don't know just what it is. I've never been able to figure it out. But no one likes me. Not even my own father." His voice broke slightly and he had to stop speaking.

"I never heard anything so ridiculous!" she cried. "Of course your father likes you! Why shouldn't he? Why shouldn't everyone like you, a fine, upstanding boy? He should be very proud to have you for a son. I would be."

He looked up suddenly, and the words came out without his willing them to, "Oh, I wish I was your son. I never knew my mother. Maybe if I had a mother like you I wouldn't be the way I am. Maybe I'd be more like Bob and Jim. Everyone likes them."

She sank suddenly into a chair and he was surprised to see tears in her eyes. "You're all mixed up about yourself," she said. "And I think I know why. And I'm going to do something about it."

"Please don't say anything to the boys," he begged. "It would only make them hate me worse."

"They don't hate you. You're so terribly wrong about things. Especially about your father. I'm sure that he loves you dearly and is proud of you."

Dave shook his head. "I'm a terrible disappointment to him. He's a very big man, you know. Important, I mean. He knows governors and senators and he's even played golf with the President."

"But he doesn't even know his own son," she said, her voice angry.

"It's no wonder he's disappointed in me," Dave admitted. "You see, I was expelled from school at the end of the term." It felt good to get this terrible thing off his chest at last.

"Expelled! Why?"

"I got another fellow to go with me and swipe four chickens. We put them in the teacher's lounge at school and they were there overnight."

"I can imagine what the place looked like the next day," she said soberly. "I don't like things like that. Jokes are jokes and we have plenty of those in the cattle country. But destruction of property is vandalism. There's nothing funny about it."

"Yes, ma'am. But we kids thought it was funny when we did it. And all our friends thought it was awfully funny when we told them about it."

She nodded, and a light of understanding came into her eyes. "That, I imagine, is the key. The real reason you do things like that. To gain attention, I believe. It's a poor way."

"So," Dave said, "when the principal asked who did it, I owned up and got expelled, even if my dad did pay for the damage. And he's hardly spoken to me since. That's why he sent me out here to get rid of me."

She shook her head. "I think you've figured things out all wrong," she said.

He got up. "I must go now," he murmured. "I've got some things to do." He picked up the packages he had brought from town. "Thanks for the cookies. I'll be seeing you."

"Wait, Dave," she called as he was going through the door. "I have something to tell you. Something you ought to know."

He again felt that terrible tightness in the pit of his stomach that always came when he thought of the item of news Windy had given him.

He turned toward her, his face tense. "I know what you're going to say," he cried fiercely. "I know already. My father's going to be married. . . ."

A look of surprise crossed her face. "You know?" she cried. "How on earth?" Then, after a pause, "That *could* be very nice for you."

"Nice!" The word came out like a pistol shot. "I hate her. Whoever she is, I hate her!"

He turned and started to run, ashamed to have Honey see the working of his face.

He heard her call after him, "Dave, wait. You don't understand. I want to talk to you." But he ran on.

He gripped the packages in his hands. He remembered why he had bought the hamburger and giant firecrackers. At the thought of his scheme, fierce anger boiled up in him. He wanted now to do something mean and terrible to ease this feeling.

He hurried across the road and tiptoed past the

clubhouse with his package of hamburger and paper sack. He heard the hum of voices inside and now and then a burst of laughter. The sound made him feel lonely and left out. Why hadn't the boys wanted him as a member? Well, they hadn't, so they could just suffer for it.

He opened his package as he walked toward the place where he had several times seen the family of skunks. Then he made a line of hamburger straight to the clubhouse and put a good-sized hunk under the opening which led underneath. This done, he looked around for a board that would cover the opening. Then he sat on a rock, hid by bushes, to wait. He hoped that the skunks were hungry. He knew that he was.

The triangle clanged its signal for dinner, but Dave did not leave. He wanted to see the fun, if any. Besides, he did not want to face the men and their embarrassing questions about why he was not with the other boys.

He did not have too long to wait. The mother skunk came, following the hamburger trail with her four little skunk children marching single file. She paused at the entrance to the hole leading under the clubhouse and Dave feared she was going to turn back. But hunger evidently overcame her better judgment. She disappeared and one by one the little ones did, too. Dave hurried forward and slipped his board in place, then put a giant firecracker inside with a long string tied to the fuse.

He ran back and lighted the string. It burned slowly along its length.

Dave chuckled. If that big bang went off underneath the clubhouse, he knew that the mother skunk would let loose her own particular ammunition.

Things went according to plan, but Dave waited only long enough to see that his string was burning well. Then he ran around to the front of the house and slid breathlessly into his place at the table just as he heard the bang.

"I stopped across the road to feed Pesky," he explained. "Sorry I'm late."

"What was that noise? Sounded like a shot!" his uncle said.

Dave had hoped to cover up the sound with his jabber.

"Probably the kids up to some devilment," Cooky said. "How come you aren't in on it?" He glared at Dave.

Dave tried to look innocent. "I went to town with Windy," he said. "Then, like I told you, I went over to feed Pesky. I brought him some oats and newfangled colt food."

"You'll have her so fat she'll have to be butchered," Windy said.

The meal was over before Randy appeared at the back door.

"Whew!" everyone cried, and hands flew to pinch nostrils together. Randy was wrapped in a horse blanket and it was plain that he was hopping mad.

"Will you give me a tub of warm water and some soap?" he asked. "I've been in the creek. Threw my clothes away. Scrubbed myself. Can't get this smell off."

"Obviously you tangled with a skunk," his father said as he brought in a washtub from the back porch and started filling it with water from the reservoir on the stove. "How come?"

"Some smart guy—and I can guess who—coaxed some skunks under our clubhouse, then blew up a firecracker, sounded like, to make them let loose. It did. Maybe about a dozen of 'em. Ruined our clubhouse. We might as well burn it down."

The men were going out of the front door to get away from the overpowering odor. Dave discreetly followed them. Slim gave him a wise look that Windy saw. "Oh, Dave's got an alibi," he said. "He was in town with me. It's skunk nature to go under buildings. Can't blame Dave."

"I suppose it's skunk nature to set off fire-crackers," Slim said.

CHAPTER XVI

To Catch a Horse Thief

DAVE had fooled no one but Windy. And he wondered if he had really fooled this wise old cowboy. Most likely Windy was just standing up for him. But his punishment was swift and uncomfortable. From the time of the skunk trick on no one spoke to him. Not even Ginny or his aunt. He was ignored as though he was not there. The men and boys talked over and around him, until he might as well have been invisible.

Three long days of it was as much as he could stand. It seemed like a year. Well, if they wanted to get rid of him, he'd oblige. He'd make them sorry they'd treated him in such a manner.

He planned things carefully. He filled a gunny sack with oats and hid it in a shed where riding gear was kept. When Cooky was away from the food storeroom he took a box of crackers and some canned goods which he put in another sack. He also took some bacon and a cold boiled potato. He had no qualms of conscience about taking these things. He planned to send the money for them later. He did not forget to include a can opener, a tin plate and cup, and a bucket and small pan to cook in. All of these things were in the storeroom and he was only borrowing them.

He had the faculty, which most people possess, if they use it, of waking himself whenever he wished. So he set his mental alarm clock for midnight and wakened on the dot.

He had piled his clothes neatly on a chair at the foot of the bed. He rose, picked them up, and stole from the room to dress in the kitchen where there would be less danger of his being heard. He did not put on his boots until he had eased himself from the back door. He tiptoed to the shed and picked up his sacks of plunder and a halter and rope and went to the corral where the horses that were used most often were kept at night. He laid down his sacks, and keeping his halter, walked out among the dozing horses looking for Homer in the moonlight.

He found the horse he was looking for, uttering a silent prayer that the horses would not become frightened and cause a commotion which would likely rouse one of the men.

"Whoa now, boys." He spoke soothingly. "It's only me. I won't hurt you. I'm your friend. Whoa there now, Homer. Be a good boy. We're going to take a trip."

He hoped that Homer would not be difficult, making it necessary to rope him. That would disturb the other horses, and anyway, Dave was none too sure of his roping ability, although he had been practicing faithfully.

But, as luck would have it, Homer was evidently still too sleepy to be full of kinks which most range horses exhibited early in the morning after a full night's sleep. He allowed the halter to be put on and submitted to being led to the fence where the saddles were. He did snort in protest and swell up when the girth was being tightened, but Dave had learned how to put his foot against the horse's side and give a forceful yank.

Then he led Homer to where his sacks were, put them behind the saddle, tossed the rope over the cantle, and swung open the gate and led Homer through. After he had closed the gate he climbed aboard and reined Homer toward the east —the place where Dave's first adventure had occurred—where he had seen that epic battle of the stallions.

He had a reason for running in this direction.

He figured that Uncle Bill and the others would think he had taken off directly for town. He remembered that Randy had pointed out a trail that would lead to the highway from the horse trap. He remembered the line-camp cabin. He planned to find this trail and ride to within walking distance of the highway. He knew that he could depend upon Homer's definite homing instinct to make him take off for the ranch as soon as he was rid of his rider. He considered that he was only borrowing this horse which had been put at his disposal, anyway.

Dave's ideas were vague as to what he would do after he reached the highway. Probably he would just let nature take its course. He dimly pictured himself as hailing some trucker—an understanding, adventuresome hero who would lead him to new excitements. But the main thought in his mind as he rode along through the night was the uproar his absence would cause as soon as it was discovered that he was gone. The thought made him chuckle. They would be sorry they had treated him so shabbily and no doubt they would each and all blame themselves and remember his many good qualities which they had overlooked when he was among them.

It gave him a ghostly feeling to be riding in the

moonlight in the middle of the night. Homer did not seem too eager for this sort of adventure and ambled along with head down.

Dave jerked impatiently on the reins and pounded his heels against Homer's sides. "Get going," he said. "We won't even be out of sight by the time the men get up for breakfast at this rate."

Homer obligingly went into a half-hearted lope.

It was a three-hour or so ride before Dave reached the line-camp cabin near the Dead Man's Gulch horse trap. He planned to stay there to rest Homer and himself before he set out on the dim short cut to the highway. He would need daylight to find it and there would not be much likelihood of hitching a ride until later in the morning. He fumbled around and found the rock and the key under it, where Randy had told him it was kept. He took care to hold the reins so that Homer would not set out on his homeward trek. But when he had the door unlocked he led the horse to a clump of trees and tied him well with the rope he had brought along. Here, he felt, the horse would be out of sight. He planned to be on his way again early in the morning.

He went into the cabin, feeling his way to the bunk bed. He knew that there were candles as well as other supplies around someplace, but he did not want to bother finding them now. There was no need. He yanked off his boots and lay down with his clothes on and pulled one of the blankets over him.

And the next thing he knew it was broad daylight. He leaped to his feet and threw open the door and looked up at the sky. The sun was well up. He glanced at his watch. It had stopped; he had neglected to wind it, but he guessed that it must be after nine o'clock.

After his first upsurge of anxiety he shrugged and thought, "Shucks, they won't have decided which way to start looking for me yet. I'll have time for some breakfast. I'm starved, and it might be a long time between meals."

After some struggles he finally managed to get a fire going in the little cookstove and soon had bacon frying. He sliced into it the boiled potato he had brought along. It made a delicious meal. He cleaned the pan and his plate, knife, and fork and put them back into the sack. Then he turned to smooth the bed he had slept on. To his surprise he saw that the upper bunk was mussed as though someone had slept in it without straightening it up.

This was strange, he thought. Slim had recently been at the line camp after mending fences. Slim would not leave an unmade bed, Dave knew. Then he looked around more carefully. There was a saucer on the window sill with a half-smoked cigar and ashes in it. Slim did not smoke. The oven door was open and there was a plate of dried-out fried potatoes and baked beans. The mice had been in the food. It was not so dried out that it had been there very long. Someone had been using the cabin recently—someone who was obviously not connected with the Rocking B, for these cowboys would not leave a line camp without cleaning up after themselves. Dave had heard this subject discussed often enough among them to know how hard and fast this rule was. Their own bunkhouse was neat and clean and each man made a habit of carrying his plate from the table and scraping the food from it and placing it in the dishpan.

Just then a wild, screaming neigh shattered the air. Dave leaped as though he had been shot. The silence had been thick enough to cut until then. He had heard that same trumpeting sound before. He was sure that it was not Homer. It reminded Dave of the golden stallion. And it might be. This was the region where he had been caught. No doubt it was the place to which he would return. But why the neigh of alarm?

Dave gathered up his belongings and locked the

door and replaced the key, then hurried to where he had concealed Homer. The horse was there contentedly grazing. He climbed the rocks behind the wild-horse pen, for this spot gave him a view for miles in all directions.

He stared around, but the country was quiet and serene, with no sign of horses or humans. He drew in a sigh of relief, yet there was a slight tinge of disappointment mixed with his relief. Maybe no one was even going to bother about looking for him. Maybe they were glad instead of sorry that he was gone.

But again that wild, trumpeting sound broke into his thought. And now it seemed to be almost beneath him. He hurried to the edge of the cliff and looked down, and there in the wild-horse trap was the golden stallion!

How on earth had he got in there again? The gate was closed tight. Then Dave remembered the evidence of the cabin recently having been occupied. Obviously someone had driven the Golden King into the pen. He was too smart to have gone in there of his own accord.

Dave's first impulse was to climb down and open the gate and give the stallion his freedom again. But on thinking the matter over he decided to lay low, and stay around and see what developed.

Surely whoever had corraled the Golden King wanted him badly—had some good reason for wanting him. He decided that Homer was concealed well enough so that no one would run across him. So he looked around for a place where he could hide out which would still give him a place where he could watch to see what happened.

He found such a spot between two boulders with overhanging shrubbery through which he could peer but where no one could see him. It was a long wait. The hours dragged. He grew thirsty and wished he had thought to bring his canteen and at least a handful of crackers.

He was about to go down to where his supplies were and get a drink and something to eat when the thud of hoofbeats caused him to draw back into his hiding place. He peered into the distance and saw a lone rider, but he was too far away for Dave to recognize him. It was probably a stranger anyway, or it could be someone looking for him. From the height of the man and the way he sat his horse, it might be Slim, but the man circled far around the wild-horse trap and disappeared among the brush. Dave decided it was merely some horseman on his way to a distant ranch. He heard nothing more and was about to come out again and go down to get food and drink when he heard the sound of a car. It was almost as noisy as Windy's jeep.

Dave stuck his head out and saw a jeep dragging a horse trailer. Riding beside it was a man on horseback. And Dave had no difficulty in recognizing this rider and his horse, even at a distance. There was no mistaking that man, the jaunty set of his black Stetson, the way he sat his horse—or the horse himself—that coal-black steed!

"Texas!" Dave breathed aloud. "What on earth are you doing here?"

At first he had the notion that Texas had come to look for him. Good old Tex! Then he remembered that Texas had quit his job to go rodeoing—probably did not even know that he had run away. And why would he be traveling alongside a jeep drawing a horse trailer?

It was not long before Dave understood the answer to this last question. The jeep was backed up until the entrance to the horse trailer was close to the gate of the horse trap. Texas opened the gate and rode inside the corral, then fixed the gate so that it was open the same width as the trailer. He rode slowly, his rope in hand. He swung the rope and his first cast caught the golden stallion around the neck.

The horse pranced on hind feet and pawed the

air but did not struggle long, for he had learned the lesson of the lariat. Texas dallied the rope around his saddle horn and tossed another loop to catch the stallion around the rump.

Dave saw what the idea was. The two ropes were being used to drag the stallion to the trailer.

He was about to leap from his hiding place and yell like a wild Indian to try to scare Texas away. Then from nowhere another rope snaked out from the side of the corral and pinioned Texas' arms to his sides and pulled him from his horse.

The other man leaped from the jeep and ran into the corral. Right away Dave recognized Wishbone. He was heading toward Texas, when a voice rang out, "Reach for the sky, Wishbone. I've got you covered."

Dave stared in the direction of the voice and saw Slim ride from behind a boulder. In his right hand he held a pistol.

Dave gave a shout of joy and ran from his hiding place. "I'm here, Slim. I'll help you."

Slim did not look at Dave as the boy ran toward him. He needed all of his attention on the men in the corral.

"I knew you were around here," he said quietly. "Have you got nerve enough to go down into the corral and tie the hands of those two hombres behind their back while I keep them covered?"

"I sure have!" Dave cried.

"Take this rope from my belt. And you can use one on Texas' saddle. Tie Wishbone first. I don't think Texas'll give us any trouble for a while. Seems like his fall knocked him out."

Dave raced down the hill and let himself into the corral. "Put your hands behind your back," he ordered Wishbone.

"Keep away from me or I'll kick your slats in," the bronc buster snarled.

"No funny business down there," Slim shouted. "My trigger finger's getting mighty nervous. Put your hands behind your back."

Wishbone did so, and Dave tied his wrists together tight.

"You're cutting off my circulation," Wishbone whined.

"Fine!" Dave said. "You'll be lucky if it isn't cut off at the neck. What do you mean stealing my stallion?"

He then hurried to Texas, who was still lying as he had fallen. It was no trick at all to twist his arms behind him and tie them. Texas was moaning slightly. As Dave tied the last knot the man moved,

opened his eyes, and stared up into Dave's eyes.
It made the boy laugh to see the look of amazement on Texas' face. He shook his head, blinked
and opened his eyes again, as though hoping that
the image he had seen would have gone away.

"Yes, it's me." Dave chuckled. "Maybe I'll string
you up for stealing my stallion."

"Whose stallion?"

"Mine. I bought him. That makes him mine."

Texas groaned and said, "Well, you certainly
bought yourself a bargain, didn't you. What good
will that devil ever do you—the dumbest greenhorn kid I ever knew?"

Dave got up from his stooping position.

"To think that I used to like you," he said. You
were quite a hero to me. And you turned out to be
an ordinary horse thief."

Texas groaned again and said, "That shows how
much you know. A wild horse is in the public do-
main. Belongs to anyone who can break and ride
him. That's the law of the range."

Dave blinked. He had never heard of this law.
It might be true. There were plenty of range laws
and things of which he was ignorant.

CHAPTER XVII

A Difficult Decision

"WHAT'RE you going to do?" Dave asked Slim.

It was strange how much confidence he now found he had in the strong, silent man. Randy was right. Slim did have loads of character. He was the man who could be depended upon in any emergency. How foolish he, Dave, had been to be so overwhelmingly impressed by the showiness of Texas—the man who, it now seemed, had turned out to be a horse thief.

Slim went over to Texas and prodded him with the toe of his boot. "Stand up," he said curtly.

Texas glowered up at the tall cowboy, but he managed to struggle to his feet.

"Go over and sit by the gatepost," Slim ordered. "You go over and sit by the opposite one," Slim told Wishbone.

Sullenly the two bronc busters stomped over

and sat down with their backs to the posts upon which the great gate swung and fastened. Then Slim went over and tied them tight to the posts.

"I reckon this will hold you until Windy and the sheriff get here."

"The sheriff!" Dave cried. "Gosh! Is he out after me?"

"It's customary when boys run away to call the sheriff," Slim said in his quiet way. "But I had a hunch we'd need him to pick up a couple of horse thieves, too."

"We didn't steal any horse." Texas glared up at Slim. "Bill Brandt didn't own this horse. The stallion really belonged to Jim Bowes. His running the range wild for two years made him anybody's horse."

"Your making up laws won't get you out of this jam," Slim told him.

Dave wondered just where he came in on this deal. He had paid for the stallion. But if it wasn't his uncle's to sell, where would he come out?

Slim calmly took the saddle and bridle from the horse that Texas had been riding and laid the saddle on the ground. He threw the bridle over his shoulder and picked up a bucket and filled it with oats and with the bucket extended walked toward the stallion. The animal's head went up. His ears perked forward and his nostrils flared. A quiver rippled through his body.

"Easy, boy, easy now!" Slim talked soothingly. "I'm your friend. You know me."

The stallion took a step forward and extended his nose, sniffed the contents of the bucket, and started eating.

Slim eased the bridle over the head between bites. Then he led the palomino close to the saddle and put the bucket on the ground. The horse went on eating while Slim threw the saddle across his back and tightened the girth.

Dave stood watching wide-eyed and with mouth open. He expected the stallion to go into one of his tantrums any minute and perhaps rear and strike Slim with sharp front hoofs. But nothing happened.

Dave heard Texas exclaim, "Well, I'll be a ring-tailed baboon!"

Slim gathered up the reins and stepped into the saddle and rode to the gate. He leaned forward to swing it wide and rode through. "Come on along, Dave. Close the gate. We'll leave our horse thieves alone to think over their sins."

Dave gave the two men a glance as he swung

the great gate shut. They were both staring at Slim on the stallion's back, their eyes bugging out, their mouths hanging open.

Dave could not restrain a chuckle at the expression on their faces, yet he was as amazed and bewildered as they were by the extraordinary turn events had taken.

Slim rode out on the prairie and the stallion broke into a beautiful gallop that was a joy to watch. Then the rider reined him into a well-executed figure eight. Again Dave gasped. It was difficult for him to believe his eyes. Could this be the same horse—the one that had been judged an outlaw, fit only for a rodeo string of buckers? Why, he was a wonder horse and the most beautiful sight Dave had ever seen!

Finally Slim reined the horse over to where Dave was standing. "Would you like to ride this fine beast?" he asked with a twinkle in his eyes.

"Me?" Dave cried.

"Sure. Keep a firm grip on the reins and let him know you're master." Slim climbed down.

Dave hesitated, but Slim gave him a nudge and he didn't have the nerve to refuse. He climbed aboard and took the reins in a firm grip and gave a slight nudge with his knees and the stallion broke into an easy, floating gallop. The feel of that tremendous power between his legs—power that he, a comparatively small person, was able to control—made him feel like a king. The wind on his cheeks, the flowing motion beneath him carrying him over the ground at such speed gave him a feeling of exhilaration that he had never known before. He felt that he would like to go on and on, it did not matter where—the end of the rainbow, the edge of the world—to mighty adventure somewhere. Then he heard a shrill whistle. The stallion's ears perked forward. He slowed and turned and galloped back to where Slim was standing.

"How did you like it?" Slim grinned impishly.

"Jeepers! What a horse! But what on earth happened? What magic did you use to tame this wild outlaw?"

Slim shrugged. "Just common horse sense. I suspected that something was up. Texas and Wishbone were piling it on too thick about the stallion being an outlaw. Then I overheard some of their conversation. Texas knew this palomino. Had broken him on the Bowes' spread two years ago. Knew he was a wonder horse as well as a beauty. He made up his mind then that this was the animal he wanted for his own. Think what a sensation he would be riding around to rodeos in all his fancy getup and on such a mount! So, a few years ago, after the horse was broken and had been given the fundamental training, Texas let him loose."

"Just the way I did?" Dave broke in.

"Yes, but not for the same reason. He figured that he'd be able to capture the palomino again someday after he'd got his full growth. Then, with just a little smoothing off, he'd have a magnificent horse. And he could always claim this unwritten law of the range—that a wild horse belongs to the one who catches and breaks him. Although I don't know whether that law would hold up in court or not."

"I'm still sort of dizzy about this whole thing," Dave said, shaking his head. "If the horse had been broken once, how did Texas and Wishbone get him to act so wild? And how did you tame him again?"

"They hokeypokeyed him," Slim said.

"Hokeypokeyed?"

"Yeh! That's carbon disulphide. A chemical that burns like fury. It sets horses crazy if it touches their skin. I happened to get a faint whiff of it once when the stallion came close to the fence near where I was sitting. That's what made me suspicious. And I noticed that both bronc busters wore gloves when they rode. I investigated Tex's gloves when he wasn't looking—found in the finger of one a little squeeze vial. They'd been filling it with hokeypokey. Simple enough to squeeze out a little through a handy hole in the end of a finger of the glove."

"I didn't know people could be so mean—so lowdown!" Dave cried indignantly.

"Oh, you'll meet all kinds in the world. But most of us are pretty good guys."

"Did you have much trouble taming the stallion again?"

"Not too much," Slim said. "I have a way with horses, you've probably noticed. And I went to work on this boy in earnest. Went out every night and talked to him. Horses like to be talked to, you know. After he was used to my voice, I got to bringing him oats, apples, sugar lumps. After I had him used to eating out of my hand, I started touching him, stroking him, lifting his feet. I got him to trust and respect me. If you get a horse to do that, the rest is easy. He'd already been broke and partly trained, you know. A horse never forgets what he's learned. I've been riding this boy around in figure eights every night for some time now."

Dave turned at the sound of a jeep approaching. "There comes Windy and the sheriff now," he said. Instantly he sobered. "Will the sheriff arrest me?"

Slim shrugged. "That's up to him. Better get down and face the music, whatever it is."

Dave climbed down. Slim took the reins and let them trail on the ground. Golden King started cropping the grass. Dave stood beside Slim, his heart beating fast as Windy and Sheriff Jones drove up beside them.

"I see you caught our runaway," the sheriff said. He wore a fierce frown.

"Not only the runaway, but also a couple of horse thieves waiting for you in the corral," Slim said. "They had the palomino stallion in there. Dave here helped me catch them."

The sheriff bent a stern look at Dave, making him shrink in his shoes. Finally he said gruffly, "Just another smart-alec juvenile delinquent, eh? I ought to take you in and put you in jail for a while and maybe teach the likes of you a lesson. But your uncle said that you were to be returned to the ranch when I caught up with you."

"A lot of trouble you put us to," Windy broke in. "Got everybody away from their work. I had to go to town and get the sheriff. We came out by way of the highway, in case you'd hitched a ride with some truck. I figgered that was what you'd be likely to do."

Slim said mildly, "Windy, why don't you let

Sheriff Jones take Texas and Wishbone to town in their own pickup? Take their horses in the horse trailer they brought to carry the palomino in. You follow the sheriff in to town in case his prisoners try to give him any trouble. Sheriff, you can put Dave in my custody. I'll take him to the ranch. We have some man-to-man talking that we can do on our way."

"Okay," the sheriff said. "But I'll see that there's a cell ready for this juvenile delinquent, if his uncle wants to send him in."

"He's no delinquent," Slim said. "Just a kid, not very sure of himself, with some mixed-up notions that he needs to get straightened out."

Dave's heart went out in gratitude to Slim for his understanding.

"I rode Homer," Dave explained, "because I knew as soon as I turned him loose he would go home. I've got him tied over there in the trees. I suppose you want to ride the stallion. We can lead the horse you rode."

"But the stallion's your horse. You bought him, you know."

"I thought I did." Dave scratched his head. "But how could I buy him if he wasn't my uncle's to sell? And how about this law of the range?"

A smile tugged at the corners of Slim's mouth.

"According to your uncle's code," he said, "the 'law of the range' doesn't hold. The stallion belonged to Jim Bowes. So when all this ruckus came out in the open, your uncle phoned Jim and arranged to buy the stallion. Sent him his check. Bowes is going out of business and was happy to sell a horse he thought he'd lost anyway."

"So the stallion's still mine?"

Slim nodded.

Dave looked at the magnificent animal, then his gaze strayed around to the hills, the rocks, the green grass.

"Maybe I'm just a sap," he said in a low voice, "but it seems to me that the stallion belongs here. Being free to gather and rule another herd. The way he did when I first saw him."

"That would mean," Slim said, "that you still wouldn't have a horse of your own. Prince doesn't belong to you. Remember? You bought this horse instead."

Dave gulped. Slim's words aroused once more in his heart that hunger for a horse of his own. Yet, Golden King lifted his head, his ears perked forward. He let out his trumpet call and it was answered by a whinny somewhere off in a fold of the country.

"Golden King belongs here," Dave said. "I can

manage to get along without my own horse. Maybe Uncle Bill will still let me ride old plug Homer."

Slim nodded as though he were pleased with Dave's decision. He lifted the saddle off the stallion, removed the bridle, and gave the horse a slap on the rump. "The world is yours, old boy," he said. "Go and claim it."

The stallion raised his head and stretched his neck and his nostrils widened as though he were drawing in deep breaths of freedom. He started trotting with high steps. Then he lowered his head and kicked out his heels and gave a joyful whinny.

"That boy will sire a lot of handsome colts," Slim said. "I'm glad you decided the way you did. I happen to know that your uncle will be in favor of what you're doing. Go get your Homer horse and we'll make tracks for home. I'll put this saddle and bridle in Windy's jeep."

CHAPTER XVIII

Dreams Come True

THE two rode along side by side in silence for so long that Dave was growing very uncomfortable. He wondered when this man-to-man talk was going to commence. He wished right now that the ground would open up and swallow him. Returning to the ranch and facing the people there was going to be the hardest thing he had ever done. What a fool stunt it had been to run away!

Suddenly Slim said, "I know just how you feel right now."

"How?" Dave asked in surprise.

"Wishing that there was some way you could miss having to face the folks at the Rocking B. You'd like to kick yourself for being such a dod-blamed fool."

"How did you know?"

A quick smile crossed Slim's mouth. " 'Cause I ran away myself once when I was a kid. Got to feeling sorry for myself. Thought I was being mistreated about something. Can't remember what. But I thought I'd make everyone sorry they were being so mean to me by running off. Having to go back and face my folks and the neighbors and the kids at school who knew I'd made such a fool of myself was the hardest thing I ever did. It hurt lots more than the licking my dad gave me."

"But everybody *was* being pretty mean to me!" Dave cried out in his own defense. "The kids weren't having anything to do with me. Then it got so no one was even speaking to me."

"The silent treatment is pretty rough medicine." Slim nodded. "But don't you think a fellow should take his medicine when he does something he shouldn't—like coaxing skunks under his friends' clubhouse, for instance?"

"I suppose so," Dave admitted. "But I wouldn't have done it if the fellows hadn't been so mean to me."

"Well," Slim said slowly, "I'll let you in on a little secret. They weren't being so mean to you. They were voting you into their club. Seems like their rules and bylaws are that anyone must do something that they consider pretty worth while before he can get in. When you gave up your own horse to buy the stallion they decided that you were

worth while. Of course, grownups might look at that stunt in a different light."

"Gee whillikers!" Dave cried. "They were voting me in! And I led the skunks under there to ruin their clubhouse. How dumb can a guy get?"

"I often wonder," Slim said mildly. "Another thing. Wouldn't it be a good idea if you knocked that chip off your shoulder?"

"What do you mean chip on my shoulder?" Dave asked.

"That means that you're always looking for trouble—for someone to slight you or treat you mean. You're touchy as a teased rattler. Just relax. Be friendly. Randy hankers to be friends with you. He told me so. But he thinks you're standoffish. I told him he was sort of that way, too. Maybe it's a Brandt trait."

"Randy wants me for his friend! And I did just about everything possible to spoil it, didn't I?"

"Just about," Slim agreed. "You've made some mistakes. Who doesn't? But listen to me, pardner. Don't ever try running away from your mistakes again. It's like trying to run away from yourself. It can't be done. Learn from your mistakes. That's the way to grow up to be a worthwhile guy. Will you remember that, pardner?"

Dave nodded. A big lump came into his throat to be called pardner by this fine man.

"Okay, then. That's the end of the lecture. Let's get into a gallop."

There was no escape from facing the people at the ranch. Dave spent as much time as possible in the corral caring for his horse, but there had to be an end to that.

"Get going, pardner," Slim finally said. "Putting it off doesn't make it any easier. Go in and face the music."

"You coming?" Dave asked hopefully.

"Nope. You did this on your own. Now take whatever medicine is coming on your own."

So Dave squared his shoulders and walked into the house through the front door. And it was just his luck that Uncle Bill, Aunt Nell, Randy, and Ginny were all in the living room. Even Honey Gail was there. And right in their midst was his father. Dave drew in his breath and his knees almost buckled under him. He stopped in his tracks. This was going to be worse than he expected.

"So," his father said in that accusing tone which Dave knew so well, "you're still up to your old tricks?"

Dave made himself look his father in the eye

and he said, "Yes, I'm sorry, sir! I didn't mean to make a pest of myself here, but I guess that's the way it turned out."

"Listen, David Brandt." Honey turned to his father and said sternly, "You remember we all held a discussion on this matter. You decided to let me do the speaking and to give out whatever punishment I thought fitting. Well, it's my idea that Dave has been punished enough. You know yourself how hard it is to have to face your family and friends after having run away. You did it yourself, I well remember. As for the skunk affair, that's the sort of thing cowmen are always pulling. Personally, I think that's going too far. I'd say that Dave must clean out the clubhouse with ashes, coal oil, and sagebrush and repaint every inch of it himself. Then we can all go on from there."

Dave gulped and stared. This punishment struck him as being fair enough and far easier than he had expected. But why was Honey handling the matter, just as though she were his mother?

His father cleared his throat. "Dave," he said in his abrupt manner, "I—we—Honey and I . . ." He stopped, then waved a hand toward Honey. "You tell him," he said.

She looked up at Dave, half-smiling. "You ran

off the other day when you had cookies at my house. I wanted to tell you then, but you wouldn't let me. And I haven't seen you since . . ." Her voice trailed off.

Dave stared at her, waiting. What was the matter? Why the big mystery? Why were his father and Honey having trouble telling him what they wanted to say?

She took a deep breath and went on. "You said that Windy had told you that your father was going to remarry. And you insisted that you hated your stepmother-to-be, whoever she was. You were so emphatic about it that you stunned me. Please don't hate her, Dave. Because I'm the one. Your father and I are going to be married. You remember that I told you we had been childhood sweethearts."

Dave gasped. "You!" It was a glad cry. "You'll be my mother! Bob and Jim and Molly and I will all be in the same family!"

Honey nodded. Her eyes were dewy.

His father cleared his throat. "Things are going to be different between us—you and me," he said. "I'm going to spend more time with you. Be a regular dad. Honey told me that you thought I'd sent you here to get rid of you. That I didn't like you. You couldn't be more wrong. I'm sorry that I've been such a failure as a father. Honey will help me do a better job from now on."

Dave sank into a chair. Never before had he heard his father admit to making a mistake. For some reason his father's new attitude made Dave's heart flood with love for this man who had heretofore been too much a stranger.

"Jeepers!" he finally said. "Will somebody please pinch me and see if I'm awake? This isn't all a dream, is it?"

Uncle Bill chuckled. "It's real. And much nicer than any dream, I'd say."

Dave's face sobered. He turned to his uncle. "Maybe I did the wrong thing again. Maybe you'll be mad at me about the golden stallion."

"What about him?" Uncle Bill asked.

"Tex and Wishbone were going to steal him. Had planned to all along. They *made* him act like an outlaw on purpose. I helped them out by turning Golden King loose. They drove him into the horse trap. But Slim came along and caught them. They're on the way to town with the sheriff now."

Uncle Bill nodded. "Slim told me that he suspected that Texas and Wishbone were up to some skulduggery. And he had a hunch that they'd likely try to use the horse trap to catch Golden King. Pretty sharp man, Slim is. But what did you do that I should be mad about?"

Dave twisted his fingers nervously. "Slim told me that you'd sent Mr. Bowes a check for the stallion, so I figured that since I'd already paid you for him, he was still mine. So I turned him loose again."

There was a silence that seemed to Dave to draw out endlessly. Finally his uncle said, "That's just what I would have done if he was mine. After Slim told me the facts about what kind of animal he really is, I decided that he's the sort created to be king of the range. But, you see, it will be my range he rules. A few extra fences will see to that. And your palomino will never know the difference. After all, he will have hundreds of acres to rule. But I'm getting the best of the deal. Do you realize that?"

Dave looked up in surprise. He had been feeling guilty about not having treated his uncle fairly.

Uncle Bill went on: "That stallion will sire some mighty fine foals. And since the mares are mine, the foals will be, too."

He chuckled, then added, "But no doubt you and I can make a deal about that. Maybe you can have your choice of the foals each spring."

"Don't forget," Dave's father broke in, "that Honey's mares will be running the same range. I think that all of us will make out all right on this deal. I'd say that Dave proved that he has very good horse sense."

Everyone nodded in agreement, and Honey beamed at Dave.

"Well, then," Uncle Bill said heartily, "now that matters seem settled to the satisfaction of all concerned, why don't you and your father mosey out and look at that Prince horse?"

"Swell!" Dave cried, jumping up. "Want to come, Dad?"

His father followed him from the room and side by side they walked to the corral fence. Dave whistled, and Prince perked up his ears, then came high-stepping toward the fence.

"Isn't he a beauty?" Dave cried. "I'm crazy about horses. And especially crazy about Prince. I trained him myself. I'll let you see him perform tomorrow."

"This is the horse I sent you money to buy?"

Dave nodded.

"But you bought freedom for the palomino stallion instead?"

Again Dave nodded, fearing his father's disapproval of this particular bit of rashness.

Surprisingly enough his father said, "I don't blame you. I think it was rather fine of you."

Dave gulped.

"Of course," the man went on, "I'll buy this Prince horse for you again."

Dave leaned his arms on the fence rail and was silent for a long moment before he said slowly, "You know, Dad, I'd rather work like the other kids do here and earn money to buy him. Then he'd really be my own. That is, if I get to come back here next summer."

He felt his father's fingers grip his shoulders. "You've done a lot of growing up this summer, son. I can see that."

Simple words those were, but they made Dave happier than he had been for a long time. Suddenly there was a bond of comradeship and understanding between father and son that had never been there before.

"You like it here on the ranch, do you, son?" The tone was warm, interested.

"Better than any place else. I wish I never had to leave."

"Good! It's like coming home to me," his father said slowly. "I'd forgotten how serene and at peace with oneself a man is in this part of the country and in this sort of life. I've decided to stay and run Honey's ranch. I have able men to run my oil business. I've made lots of money, but got ulcers doing it."

"You mean—we'll live here all the time? I won't have to go back to the city to school?"

"Honey's ranch will be our permanent home. We have a whole family."

"Wow!" Dave cried.

"You and I will work together. We'll be partners. You can learn the horse business while you are growing up."

They turned and walked slowly back to the house. There was no need for more words. Understanding linked them together.

That night when Dave went into Randy's room to go to bed, he thought that his cousin seemed to act withdrawn and distant.

Finally, when he was about to pull the covers up, Dave blurted, "Did you ever know such a lucky guy as I am? I've been pretty pesty around here and I suppose I should be locked up, but here I've got a whole nice family all of a sudden, or will have soon. And will get to live on a ranch and have horses around and everything all hunky dory."

"You *are* lucky," Randy said in a quiet tone.

"What's the matter with you? Are you still sore about the skunks? That was pretty mean. I'm awfully sorry and I promise to get the place smelling like roses."

"It's not that." Randy looked away.

"Then what's eating you? Is it because of our quarrel about Slim and Texas? You were right and I was so wrong. I turned out to be a lousy judge of a real he-man."

"It wasn't that," Randy said in a strained voice. "It's—well—you'll be living across the road. Bob and Jim will be in the same family with you. Where will that leave me?"

Dave gasped. So that was it! He sat down on the bed beside Randy. "They'll be my half-brothers," he said. "But you know how brothers are. Mostly they fight a lot. I'd like to have you for my best friend forever."

"You would?" A glad light came over Randy's face. "Gosh! That's what I've wanted. But you were so sort of standoffish. I thought you didn't like me."

"And I thought you were standoffish and didn't like *me*. Slim says our families are all alike that way. Standoffish, I mean. Gosh! All my life I've wanted a best friend like you. And all of a sudden here you are."

Both boys stuck out their right hands and clasped them tight and hard in a wordless pledge of eternal friendship.

Dave went over and climbed into bed. "You know, don't you," Randy said, "that we voted you in the Top Handers. That's the name of our club. That's what the T H C brand on our clubhouse door means. We were voting you in when you skunked us."

"Slim told me. I thought that I queered myself for good when I skunked you."

Randy shook his head. "We haven't voted you out, so you're still in," he said. "I reckon if you get the place unstunk, you'll still be a member all right."

Dave pulled the covers up under his chin and gave a great sigh of happiness.